Melancholy's Web

Zach Miller

First Edition
Copyright © 2020 by Zach Miller
ISBN: 979-8-9880760-1-8

For those who love us and those we love.

And those who don't love us anymore.

Mary Beth and the Lonely No More

Mary Beth in a muumuu (floral print), aged 28 and jagged-toothed, insulated by about eighty pounds more than her petite frame was comfortable supporting, walked into her room, placed a package on her work table, and scratched the turkey waddle on her mole-dotted neck with a delightful smile on her face.

There was precious little time to waste. She tore away the outer paper and ripped open the cardboard shipping box as she would a candy wrapper. After brushing the detritus into her tableside waste bin, she looked lovingly at the treasure ready to make her heart's fondest dreams come true.

The smooth, pinewood box said LONELY NO MORE.

Her plump sausage fingers—nearly free of lines—made whispers over the bare finish of the lid, tracing playfully over the ridges of each letter. The outside, in her quivering gaze, was perfect. So wonderful that the thought of revealing its contents brought fear bubbling from the innards as the fear of approaching perfection from a distance to reveal the fast decaying nature of a wonderful dream.

But this was no dream. It was a gateway to the dream, and the only way was forward.

The buttered silk hinges uttered no sound or resistance as her pudgy digits lifted then placed it delicately on the table. Obscuring the cargo within was a simple white slip with a face of Inria Serif font.

Dear Lonely Dreamer,

You stand at the doorway to happiness and fulfillment. It's time to say goodbye to a cold and cruel world that refuses to recognize your talent and value. Don't waste another moment being sad or downtrodden. Inside this box is the key to fully realizing your most wondrous fantasies with the Lonely No More from Collywobbles Cabinet. Before you are four blocks of White Pine with a red ribbon supplied for each. In the tray beneath are your utensils. Do not lose a single piece, as they are each irreplaceable. Put the entirety of your heart into every moment and visualize your desires as you work. When your efforts are finished, tie a ribbon around each one while saying a prayer for that which you fervently desire. Follow the steps carefully and exactly. A job left unfinished is a job not believed in. Believe with all of your might and watch the garden of sublime joy bloom in your life.

Godspeed, Dreamer. And thank you for choosing Lonely No More.

What began as the pursed lips of concentration spread into a jagged fault line of a smile, which gaped like a fracture across her plump head.

Curved over her table in the shape of a fishhook, she reached with tender care into the box when her mother's shrill voice warbled down the hall, bounced from wall to wall, and entered her ears, which had been enjoying the blissful silence of her concentration.

"Come eat, babeh girl!"

She whipped her head at the doorway with the sneer of a junkyard dog. Mary Beth was a woman oft irritable who enjoyed getting lost in her fantasies, but never before had she been so livid at the slight of interruption. However, the gravelly purr of an empty stomach drained the rictus of firmity and her face returned to its zaftig volume.

"So hungry," she whispered, rubbing her tummy in soft little circles. "Soon," she said, closing the lid on the box with the careful motions of a jewel thief, "I need to be at full strength."

Her mother's voice again; "Mary Beth?"

"I'm comin', Momma!" she called, and hurried out of her room.

For the next two weeks, Mary Beth worked slowly, carefully, and in secret as if her life depended on it. Perhaps it did, for hers was a life of lonely function, a familiar and awful curse which only meaningful work could abate.

Eating, for all she did, did not abate the loneliness. Television did not abate the loneliness. Reading did not. Sleeping did not. She awoke from dreams of sorrowful joy to a reality of petrifying *emptiness*.

Of *sameness* that chewed at the frayed edges of the soul.

But all of that was going to change. She was going to change it.

To aid in this most important endeavor, she had retrieved from a lockbox beneath her bed a collection of her most cherished memories. Yearbooks, photos, old letters, all sad reminders of time and people she wanted back. She pinned what she could of these precious things above her workspace, taking moments to remind herself of all that was dear and decent in her past and future. Her body, though small in stature and far too heavy, had an urge to live for others, and held a fragile, endangered heart full of so much love to give it spent nights trying to tear away from her chest.

That's what Momma had always told her.

"Please don't cry, mah sweet lil' girl. Yer heart's not strong because it beats too hard for others and not enough for isself. It jess wants'a fly right outta yeh and let e'ryone know it's there. Shh, don't cry. Issall gon' be all raht as long's yer here with yer Momma. Momma loves yeh so much."

And Momma did love her. Sometimes too much.

Most times too much.

It was a love that could elevate and choke in the same mighty gust. Though Mary Beth would never say it to her dear mother's face (oh Lord, no, not to sweet Momma who'd always been there and watched after her and kept her from the meanness of the world), she sometimes resented the love and affection with which her mother had used as a blanket to keep her swaddled from infancy. She often thought through the years that she could *do more, go more, be more,* if maybe Momma just didn't love quite *so much.*

But in the end, she knew that would be ungrateful, and she didn't want to hurt Momma.

Even when Momma's love sometimes hurt her.

While she was bent over in diligent precise work, the work of great importance to the well-being of her heart and soul (and how far she had come since the beginning!) her dear, wonderful, sweet, loving, suffocating Momma came waddling up down the hall with a wheezing huff after shouting her lungs weak, worried darn near sick that her beautiful baby *again* didn't want to come out of her room for *brickfiss.*

"Mary Beth, *what're* you doin'!"

"Not now, Momma, please."

"But what're—"

"I'm busy, Momma! This is important." Mary Beth said, her voice breaking, tears beginning to well up in her eyes. "Dammit!" she cursed under her breath, quickly wiping away the first blurs in her vision.

Her Momma looked up at the old photos and stationary she had pinned to the wall and spread among her room, her eyes opening wide with concern.

"This has sumthin tuh do with why yer in here all day bein' so quaht, innit? Wha's goin' on, Mary Beth."

"Nothing, Momma. I'm—*sniffle*—I'm working! That's all. I'm just workin'!"

"But yeh've only been in here carvin' away at...well, what *are* those thangs, Mary Beth? They don't even look lahk people. More'n lahk yer carvin' lil angels er sumthin'.'"

"Maybe I am. They are angels," she said softly. "My angels."

She handled each piece with the gentleness of a mother with her newborn.

"Babeh girl, I don't like this. Now come'own outta this room, y'hear meh?"

"I can't, Momma. I have to finish." Tears had begun rolling freely from Mary Beth's eyes. All the sadness of secrecy and hurt and hearing the concern in her mother's voice was too much to contain. "I have to finish for them. For *me!*"

"Mary Beth, I'm scared nah! Why do yeh have all these...these *pitchers* spread around yer room! They ain't nuthin' but old ghosts!"

"They ain't ghosts, Momma! They're *real! They're alive out there in the world while I'm stuck here with you! Because my heart's not strong! Because...because I'm not strong!*"

Her cheeks were as shiny and swollen as a balloon in the rain. Tears streaked down in seamless rivers, curving round and taking shelter beneath the quivering mounds before losing purchase to the forces of gravity and falling upon her trembling bosom.

"If I'd been a better friend, Momma! If I'd done better! If I'd been stronger! They'd still be with me! They'd—they'd still love me!"

"*I* love yeh, Mary Beth, and I'm worried bowtch'eh!

"I didn't try hard enough, Momma! If only I'd done more!"

"Babeh girl, now you're just weavin' melancholies. People'r gonna come and go in lahf."

"But nobody's ever come to me!"

"Sometimes that's for the bes', baby. People will lie to yeh and hurtch'eh and bleed you drah. You gotcher Momma, and I would'n t'ever do nothing like that to yeh. The world and the people out there ain't worth cryin' over."

"Momma!"

"Stap it right nah, Mary Beth! I'm worried, y'hear? Yer makin' yer momma awful worri'd. You know you ain't got a strong heart. This stress could kill yeh!"

"I don't care, Momma! I want my friends back. I want to be happy!"

"Well...I don't think you could take that right now, punkin," her mother said with tears in her own eyes. Her voice had fallen right off a cliff. "Happiness could kill yeh, too."

For a moment the older woman looked at her fat, weeping child.

"I just woahnna protech'eh, baby girl. C'mon and get sum ta eat."

"I'm don't wanna eat, Momma."

10

"Now enuff'a this! I said come'n eat!"

Mary Beth looked up with a terrible anger in her face that scared her mother so badly, the old woman reeled back in shock.

"I'm not hungry!"

The wail was so powerful, so full of bitter enmity; her mother took two stumbling steps back into the hallway, tears now spurting down her own fat, pink cheeks. Mary Beth sprung from her seat faster than her heavy frame should've been able and slammed the door closed.

For many long moments there was only the dreadful silence like the utterly empty space following a clap of thunder.

"Oh baby, baby, baby..." came the quiet sobs through the door, but Mary Beth didn't hear them. She was on her bed, the half-finished pieces of the Lonely No More clutched to her chest, weeping herself to sleep.

From then on she worked; worked to the hiss of sweet promises made by blades on wood, worked to the music of her mother's crying from the kitchen, worked to the frantic rhythm of pounding thunder-drums in her heart. Not eating, barely sleeping; the bloated sausage skin of her cheeks had taken on the stretched appearance an empty bag. Fleshy bowls collected dust beneath her eyes, which took the random teardrop as a desert drinks the rain.

Many times she almost faltered and declared them finished in her clamant need, but in remembrance of the dire importance of her work, she forced her hands to steady and her eyes to dry so that she may carry on with precision. The arduous journey to the end was fraught with concern and fear but never doubt. Even the jagged edges of the fear was chipped and smoothened by the waves of faith surging from her loving heart until all that remained was the Dreamer and the Dream.

At the end...finally...at *long, long* last, Mary Beth with her bloodied, calloused hands and dehydrated body (so tired but less burdened by about fifteen pounds) gathered her infant angels clad in their silky red ribbon swaddles, lifted them from the workspace womb and delivered them to their loving home. She carried them across the room and swung open the outer wall of a gorgeous vintage dollhouse that had once belonged to her grandmother, and placed each of the little wooden carvings in their own personal rooms, saying a prayer for each as her final work neared its end.

"Christina, my best friend and big sister. I love you so much. I always wanted to be just like you."

The theater girl and valedictorian. So strong. So smart and talented. Even with her lithe frame, sharp looks, and signature jet-black bob, Mary Beth had always fancied that they could've been mistaken for siblings. Chris had been her hero, always looking out for her from a distance.

"Benny, my only guy friend. So funny. You could always cheer me up whenever I was feeling down. I've needed to laugh like the old days for so long."

Henny Bo Benny, shaggy-haired and so carefree. He and his friends saw her crying on the way from the bathroom after trying to make herself throw up after lunch. When they were about to lay into her, he was the one that said she wasn't worth it, saving her so much embarrassment. Then he said he didn't like the food either and it made her snort.

"Charlotte, you were always so very beautiful. I still remember when you gave me fashion tips when I was having a hard time. You told me I should go to the prom even when I didn't have a date, or I might always regret it. You were right. I'm so glad I went. It was the most magical night and you were so gorgeous. Like the princess I always wished to be."

The platinum-locked homecoming queen. Even though Mary Beth knew that being nice to the little people was what every good queen did, she always felt that she and Charlotte connected.

"Eric...m-my high-school sweetheart. Not a day passes that I don't think of you. I came to every game I could, just for you. Even when it was too cold or too hot and Momma didn't want me to go, I fought to come see you play. I'll never forget the dance we shared. You're the love of my life and always will be."

The tall, sandy-blonde haired quarterback. She sat behind him in several classes and said good morning to him with a smile every chance she could. The days he looked her way were the most magical days she had ever known. When Mary Beth had showed up to prom in that hideous old dress (the only thing her mother had the fabric to stitch together) the group had crowded together, across the gymnasium from where she sat alone, and she would have sworn the gates of Heaven swung open when she looked up to see him walking straight towards her. He held her like she was made of brittle glass and the slightest touch or even being too close could cause her to shatter in her itchy gown.

She fell to her knees before the dollhouse, hands clasped together in prayer of contrition. "I love you all so very much. I know you've all been so, so busy, but I miss you so badly I feel like I might die from it. My heart has never been the same without you all in my life. I've felt so terribly empty and alone. Please, please, please come back to me. Please, please come back to me. Please, please come back to me."

She genuflected and prayed so hard for so long, her poor head became light and fluffy as a feather and she stumbled back against her bed, sobbing. "Please, please, please..."

"*Whummbbgg.*"

An impossible sound made Mary Beth glance with teary eyes around her room. All was seen through blurry window eyes, but the sound in her ears was the somnolent, flappy-lipped mumbling of someone emerging from repose.

"H-hello?" Mary Beth said...and when she looked back at her treasures, all the air *oomphed* from her lungs and her hands flew to her mouth.

The blunt, wooden carvings were gone, and in their places were four perfect little people, each with a lovely red ribbon tied around their torso.

Mary Beth blinked, wiped her eyes until they hurt, uttered a crazed giggle, wiped again, then looked; and they were still there.

She pinched her cheek like she imagined person dreaming would do if they realized they were dreaming, but the image before her did not flee or alter.

It was real.

Benny was a distant cry from the boy she'd known, but his soft face and sharp eyes were still there under an overgrown bush of hair and five-o'-clock shadow. He was dressed in baggy and disheveled clothes like he'd been on the road. And that made sense. Last she had heard, he was going on tour with his band. He probably never received any of her letters. That was why he didn't write back. She knew sweet Benny would have written back if only he could.

His head was down like the rest of them. His eyes, fluttering.

Gorgeous Charlotte. Her blonde wonder had faded slightly and the weight of motherhood and too many cocktails packed her sweater and jeans, but Mary Beth saw her fantastic smile and gentle wave as she always had. She was still that elegant princess.

Christina, ever lovely as the morning light, was dressed in a sharp suit like one of those lady lawyers in Momma's TV shows. Her black hair was a little longer, but still straight at a spill of oil. It shined almost blue in the light. Her face wore the lines of adulthood with bravery, but she was still every bit the supermodel Mary Beth had always adored.

And Eric...beautiful Eric. If only he'd been in a tuxedo, like the night they'd danced. Oh...her heart couldn't have taken it. He was in simple pajamas. His body was as full and strong as ever. Even a receding hairline couldn't rob an ounce of class from his dashing looks. Just seeing him again brought a well of tears to the surface.

"What...the...hell?" Benny's eyes were open, his head rolling from side to side, taking in the room of which he was now an occupant. "I knew it. I *goddam* knew it! They said I'd be sorry if I started shooting up."

"Benny!" she snort-laugh-cried at once, jolting the others. "*I can't believe i-i-i-t!*" Her voice was bursting out in rolling waves of stifled sob-laughter, punctuated by the pops of snot-shined lips.

"What's going on?" Charlotte cried. Her hands were already rubbing her body up and down, attempting to index that for which her mind could not account. "Why can't I move my legs?"

"Charlotte! I can't—I can't believe you're here! Stay calm, okay? Everything's okay."

"Mary—Mary Beth?" Christina said, rubbing stars into her disbelieving eyes. "This is a dream. This isn't real."

"It's real, Chris! And it's wonderful, isn't it!"

Charlotte began screaming, beating her fists against her head in a desperate attempt to bring some sanity back to herself, to rescue herself from the Hell into which she'd stumbled.

"Char Char, stop! What are you doing? *Stop!*"

"Shut the hell up!" Benny shouted. "I've got a splitting headache."

"Benny?" Christina called. She was in the room to the left of his own, situated so that she could just see him through the adjoining doorway. It was then that she began tugging at the red ribbon and rubbing at her legs. "Benny! Why can't we move?"

"Because I'm high as shit and probably in a coma right now."

"No!" Mary Beth squeaked. "No! It's okay. You're all okay, see? You're just right here with me. I know you're scared. I'm a giant to all of you right now, but it's okay! Nothing's going to happen. I'm right here. You're all right here."

Christina glanced around quickly, taking in all that she could, still unconvinced any of it was real. All of them were. Who could blame them? "Benny...and Charlotte? Who else is here?"

"Oh my God." The words were finally uttered by Mary Beth's tall, handsome knight.

"Eric!" Christina called.

"Wake me up now! Right now!" Charlotte screamed.

"Yeah. What the hell is this? Am I dead? If I wake up, I'm suing my pharmacy for all they've got. They gave me something *bad*."

Mary Beth, in a frightful, deliriously happy yet confused daze, rocked back and forth on her knees, hands knotted against the saggy tube of her neck, watching her friends talk and figure things out like a soap opera, like the old days, like the thing she'd dreamed of for so very long. Seeing them again.

"Mary Beth?" a muffled voice drifted through her closed door.

"Oh my God. Momma!" Mary Beth cried out, eyes bulging wide. She sprang to her feet on numb legs and stumbled to her door.

"Mary Beth!" Christina tried in vain to capture the girl's attention.

A few moments later, Mary Beth returned, tugging her Momma by the soft, doughy arm. She pulled her in front of the dollhouse and presented with a sweep of the hand "Look! It's magic, Momma! I know you never really believed but I did what you told me. I always believed it was real!"

"Real what, babeh girl? Yer little dolls? Yeh did a good job on 'em, punkin-face."

"Can't you see 'em, Momma?" Mary Beth looked back and forth from the dollhouse to her mother's face. "Why can't you see 'em?"

She looked to her friends to help, and she saw them in all their beauty. They were as silent and still as if they really were made of wood, frozen in the poses they'd been in moments before. In her own compromised vision, however, what Mary Beth couldn't see was the tears running down their faces.

Her Momma, all concern and love for her sweet, fragile child clear as day in her face—all the love in the world—just looked at the collection of crudely carved wooden pieces, then put a hand to her daughter's cheek. "Well...maybeh I don' need tuh see 'em, sweet pie. If they make yeh happy, that's all't matters."

Mary Beth clasped her hands beneath her chins. "I think you're right, Momma. That must be it. Nobody else needs to see them. They're mine. It's just for me..." Her voice trailed off into a whisper as she looked on, entranced by her thoughts of a special power that somehow only she commanded. "Oh, thank you, Momma!"

"Babeh, I juss wish I knew wha's goin' on witch'eh."

"Nothing, Momma, nothing! Everything's perfect."

"You need't eat sumthin'!"

"I will! I promise." She pushed her mother with gentle urgency across the room and out the door. "I'll be out in just a little bit, okay? I just want to tidy up some. I love you, Momma! I love you so much and things are going to be better from now on!"

"I love yeh, too, sugar pie. I just—" The door closed slowly and Mary Beth returned to her friends, which were suddenly moving and talking like normal again.

Christina's calm had been blown to bits. "Oh my God, oh my God. Oh *shit!*"

"What was that? Why couldn't we move?" Benny said, suddenly sober. Awfully, terrifyingly *sober*. "Why couldn't I talk?"

Charlotte and Eric had gone nearly catatonic.

Christina pushed back her hair and took several deep breaths. "Okay, okay. There has to be a reason for this. How did this happen?"

"I brought you here, Christina? I did it. I got the package, I did the work, and I *made* this happen! Isn't it *amazing?*"

"What did you do, Mary Beth? What package?"

Mary Beth grabbed the box and showed them. Her shaking hands lost grip and the box at utensils spilled to the floor, the slip of paper landing face up. "I was expecting a pack of paintbrushes, but the package looked too big, and I—I order a lot of craft, you know? I remembered sending for a free gift a few months ago. When I read it...I knew right away it was something special. Don't you see? I believed!"

"But what did you *do?*"

"It was a carving kit! I read the note and followed the instructions exactly. I carved the dolls and tied the ribbons around them and said my prayers and I *believed!*"

"What is that paper there? Is that the directions? What does it say?"

"I think I'm gonna be sick," Benny belched.

"Shut up, Benny! What does it *say*, Mary Beth?" Christina demanded.

Mary Beth plucked up and paper and began to read it aloud, then frowned. "It...it didn't say this before. It's changed." She was silent, her lips sounding the words to herself again to be sure she didn't miss a thing.

"What does it *say!*"

She snapped to attention. "Nothing! It just says that no one else but me should handle you. That it's important to care for you with all my heart and I do! Momma saw you as wooden dolls. I bet that's what everyone would see. You're safe in my room and Momma would never touch my things. It's okay. Please calm down."

"Don't let her come back!" Benny shouted.

"I guess...I guess now you all know how much it hurts to be invisible."

"Mary Beth..."Christina looked sick to her stomach while Eric was violently shaking his head.

"I'll take care of you," the chubby woman said with tears welling up.

Christina seized up. *"You can't fucking take care of us! We're people, not things! We're not your fucking toys!"*

"Why are you being so mean!" Mary Beth screamed through the filter of a tear-choked throat. "Look at all I've done to get you here! Isn't this magical? Isn't it incredible? People go their whole lives looking for real magic in the world and you see it right here and...and...you want to run away from it because it's me. Why does everyone want to run away from me!"

"Oh God." Charlotte's head lolled. "I think I'm about to faint."

"Good," said Eric. "When you wake up from this nightmare, call me and get me out of here, too."

Mary Beth sniffled and ran a wrist under her snotty nose. "You...you two stayed in touch?"

"We all still talk. Not as much with Benny and Chris, but he's on the road a lot and she works—" he stopped himself, suddenly aware that he was talking to a giant fat woman as he was stuck in a dollhouse like it was an everyday *damn conversation!*

"I'm ready to wake the hell up now!" Benny roared.

"Why...why didn't you ever write me back? Or call? Why are you all acting like this? I've waited *so long* to see you again! While you left and left this town and left me and my feelings to…to *rot here*! None of you ever even cared about me, did you? *Did you? I loved all of you so much and you couldn't wait to forget that I exist!*"

Benny's eyes went wide. "What the hell do you want, huh? Weren't we nice to you? It was high school. Grow the hell up and get your own life! You want to sit in here all day by yourself playing with crap and expect…expect people and happiness and love come to you! Wake up, Mary Beth! *Wake the hell up and let us out of here right now!*"

"*Stop it!*" Mary Beth screamed.

"Shut the hell up, Benny!" Christina barked. "You're scaring her! She doesn't deserve this. Mary Beth, I'm sorry. Okay? We're all sorry. But you have to let us go, now! You have to fix this, okay? Fix it!"

Mary Beth backed away, shaking her head in denial. She plopped her butt onto her bed and sat there, a waterfall of tears. "No. No. No. I didn't want this. I just want somebody to care!"

"Listen…Mary Beth. The truth is, uh," Christina looked around, searching for some sense of understanding from her fellow captives. "The truth is we were going to get in touch with you soon! All of us. It was a plan. We've talked about you ever since high school. We were just finding time in our schedules to—"

"To what?"

"Tooo…to come see you! We were all going to make the trip to visit and see you. We're going to take you out. Dinner, dancing.

Anything you want. Just reconnect like old times. Doesn't that sound great?"

"You were? Oh my God, Chris."

"We were!" Eric nodded vigorously. "We're so sorry. We should have called and told you. We've all just been so busy and things get put off, you know? And that's not right."

"No! No! It's okay. I understand." Mary Beth smiled a smile bigger and brighter than any before.

Tears fell like rain drops on her chest.

"I'm so happy for all of you, truly. I'm so so—" suddenly dizzy, she clutched her chest and sat down, trying to shake away the rush of overwhelming joy spreading through her every inch.

"So just let us go, okay? And we'll all call—well we'll just come here as soon as we wake up or get back or whatever. Just don't bring us back like this, okay? You have to promise."

"I know. I wouldn't. Oh my God, this is so incredible. I need to sit for a minute." Mary Beth swayed and giggled like a delighted schoolgirl. "Momma was right, my heart can't take this happiness!"

She shook her head. So tired all of a sudden.

"Come on. Get up. You need to let us go right now, Mary Beth. We'll all be here soon, okay?"

"I will. I will. I just—"*gulp*"—I need to rest for a minute, please? Just a minute. Just let me rest a second and look at all of you. We're going to make so many great memories, but I want this one with me forever. Like snapshot for my heart. Oh, my heart's so full right now."

"Mary Beth, get up!" Christina shouted, her composure sloughing off again. "Get up right now and let us out of here!"

"I feel so weak…just let me rest…please. I love you all so much."

"Don't you dare go to sleep! Don't you dare!"

Mary Beth, so plump and content and brimming over with affection for someone to have and appreciate and hold dear, slumped back and curled up on her bed, never once taking her tearful eyes off the most wonderful people she'd ever known. People that she believed would now be a part of her life again. Chris screaming now but it was so far away, drowned out by the rush of happiness closing all around. Closing around like beautiful, endless light.

"Mary Beth!"

Mary Beth lied down and drifted.

Drifted with her friends in her teary sight.

Drifted with happiness bursting from her heart.

Drifted away…with a smile on her face.

Hope Lies at the Bottom

I've heard it said that all roads lead home, that rivers flow to the ocean, that you can run from the past but not escape it. I doubt all of that is strictly true. Hell, I don't even know what some of it means, but I shiver in a cold, creeping sheath of sad terror when I dwell too long on the fundamental core of that dreadful idea. In a word, fate. That each of us could be so controlled, directed, limited, whatever, by forces outside of our control that—well, I don't need to expound on the oversimplified yet perfectly understood and eloquently phrased concept of Shit Happens. As the phrase drives home, it's really pretty straightforward.

The whole world learned all it needed to about that when it happened. Whatever the hell *it* was.

Is that a good way to start an awful story? I don't even know. There are no beginnings or ends anymore. You don't just wake up to some fresh pain and get the first ache of the day in your bones and get that first bit of mud on your shoes. That's the sort of day you can look forward to ending. Coming home no matter the shit that's stuck to you, peeling off your clothes for a hot shower (if one was so fortunate) and having some dinner before falling into bed.

No matter the exhaustion, the utter emptiness of all will and strength within you, you never experience a full sleep with the weight of the cold earth pressed against your side and pain from the days before rolling like slow thunder over your fetus shape and the mud, sweat, blood, come, and tears stinking up your body as your only blanket.

The End, for those cursed enough to survive in it. That's what I'm talking about.

I doubt I'll ever meet a new person in this swollen membrane of Hell that will be fresh enough to educate about what once was. That's good. I couldn't explain if I wanted to because no one knows. People have speculated in the firelight of cold evenings, hugged to the flame against the whipping chill, but I don't think we'll ever grip firmly anything but empty guesses. If I had to stuff it all into a nasty nutshell, it went something like this.

The roads were blasted to greasy black smudges as the trees bent toward them in mourning, all spiraled down like burnt matches.

The buildings looked like flowers blooming in reverse, talon curves of wire petals twisted in on themselves. I imagine how strong and brave they must've looked against a sky on fire.

The wind was like the wailing of the world and it brought blood crying from the ears. I hadn't heard a howl so fierce since my first broken heart.

Families bowed their heads together and were blown apart from charred huddles to dusty bits. People were rent asunder, dissected like detritus in a great storm, and all at once everyone was alone.

Sorrow marched like a womb of maggots in the calamity after. Mothers with dead babies and people with dead pets and men with dead hearts shrieked and opened their throats with still smoking shrapnel. Bodies folded to the earth and their heads poured back to let the rats rush in. Hollow husks without the will to die picked at the remains.

Even an idiot like me would know what happened next. After the world awoke to its worst nightmare. I could tell it or skip it. It doesn't really matter. It's only natural to think the women and children had it worst. In some ways that's true, but if you ask me, I think the weak mean had it worst. They always do. If you've ever been struck with a lightning bolt of cold, impotent failure straight through the heart, imagine it frozen in time under the whistle of a blade or club while your tear drenched, blood-spattered loved ones look on.

The savage shadows of men washed over the crumbs of creation in a violent wave. They toiled day and night, making steel gardens of fleshy bodies. The weak inherited terror, shrieking at the mercy of the strong, and the dark corners of escape brimmed with frightened and lonely suicides, and the streets gurgled with blood.

That was the death of the world.

How did I survive? Just unlucky.

But enough of the bready exposition. Let us get to the meat.

We were strung together by chains, drug along through the retch and decay. Tin cans on a bumper, led like chattel behind a caravan that pushed on through the end in a parade of death, down long dead roads reduced to spiky shards, through the bones of towns picked clean.

Two wagons, a flatbed truck that ran like a half-dead beast, and a few rusting motorcycles. On the flatbed were large animal cages that held the captive women. The stronger men pulled the wagons and those like me trailed behind to push the truck through mud or incline.

My new masters, captains of filth and cruelty, had an assortment of tributes to vulgarity as their namesakes. Even if I remembered half of their ridiculous titles, I would only speak them if necessary. A name was an honor given to the important, and I swore never to give them a space in my thoughts. What little left I had that was clear was reserved for memories I would not forsake.

The name of my current personal possessor had to be known and respected, however, for the sake of my own survival. He was called Skullfucker, amusingly enough. Not terribly original, but I guess originality doesn't mean much in a world where you take what you want from those you can kill. Apparently, there were two other Skullfuckers but he killed them and fucked their skulls. At least he was dedicated to the moniker.

In the soft, piddling mediocrity of my previous life I tended to the sick and dying, and he claimed me for my delicate nature and medical acumen. In the ravaged, nightmare-fueled fever dream world through which we walked, people were as much a commodity as food or potable water, and he considered me an investable conquest, the spoil of a bloody gang battle, though even that didn't mean I would live long.

Despite my overwhelming exhaustion from running, my abject terror at the hell in which I'd found myself, and feeble-attempts to resist, he took me violently on the first night and many nights after. Even once I'd learned to go limp, to open myself like a devoted lover, he delighted in my slug-trail of tears and puppy-yips of pain. For months, I lied on the ground beside his mat like a dog at night, curled up and pulling the dirt and frailty of dreams over me as familiar arms. After a time of his cruelty and protection, I came to deprive an odd sense of comfort from his strength. The creeping insanity of dependence. Even when I first began to send out trembling, icy fingers to graze the hardened muscle of his back and he turned and kicked my ribs so hard I thought they might cave in, I still yearned for the comfort of closeness. If he cursed me, it was *something*. If he hurt me, it was *something*!

After a time, he allowed me to indulge my weak desires without retribution. When it was coldest, and the winds howled and our little cloth tent nearly fell upon us. Maybe a part of him was scared, too. He was a pernicious monster with no heart, more a ruthless slab of stone than man, but fear and loneliness do wondrous, awful things to us all. I imagine even he was thankful that someone shivered beside him in the savage void of the left behind road.

We caravanned up a meth-nightmare road in the twisted backwoods of a nowhere place, funneled along between the charred and dead remains of everything. If the dead sky through the lattice of blackened branches had been an oil painting, I would have titled it A View of Hopelessness. Maybe too derivative.

We came to a lane of pulverized gravel between two rows of paint-faded tombs, roofs bowed and shutters dangling like fake eyelashes cried loose. I was surprised to see so many things still standing, but I was sure they wouldn't stand long.

Our convoy came to a halt and my owner, sitting on the back of the flatbed, flicked his wrist while holding the chain to my collar. It whipped up and hit my brow with a jingling *pop* and he called my name, or one of the many epithets associated with me.

"Time to make yourself useful."

I undid my fastenings and followed him up to the house. The drill was familiar by now; I was the canary. The meat shield. I went in first and notified the rest of safety. The walls inside were gravid and soft with the same turbid water that pooled on the hardwood floor. I took tentative steps onto boards that I hoped weren't too rotten to suspend my weight. Thankfully, the house didn't seem ready to collapse, thought time would soon tend to that. The kitchen was a haunting gallery of open cabinets, bare to all but the dullest of sight. A few cans of beans and black olives stood on a shelf in the pantry, but what was left of a bag of molded rice lay strewn across the floor with rat shit.

"Come on," my master said while others checked the upper floors. "Waste of goddamn time."

"Don't you want to check the rest of the place?"

"What the hell you think we're lookin' for, dumbass? Think you'll find food in the couch cushions?"

"Might be a basement."

He was silent a moment, then, "Fine. Long as we're here. But be quick about it."

We searched the rest of the first floor and found a door in the living room, full of cool, dry air. There weren't stairs within, but a storage room that wasn't terribly deep. Within, however, was a hinged door in the floor.

"Hell, you're not such a dick-brained piece of trash every damn day, now are ya? Since you called it, be my guest."

"Storm shelter?" I wondered aloud. "Haven't seen many basement doors like that."

"Only one way to find out."

I stooped to open it and found it would only lift about half an inch. "It's tied up here, from the inside. Someone probably crawled in for a safety and died. I need to cut through it."

He tossed me one of his knives, a cunning little hook blade with a deadly edge. "You know the drill. You can take it down there in case somebody's waitin', but you're gonna place that back in my hand when you're done. If any other thought passes through your soggy cow patty of a mind, think good and hard about the next thing you want goin' through your ass."

"I've never disobeyed you. Why would this time be any different?"

"I see it your eyes, you little shit. You're gettin' desperate or goin' crazy. Don't know which. Don't really matter. I don't give a damn how long you live. Bein' my property and all is the only reason I'll grant a small kindness. Think about how bad you might die."

We stared at each other for a moment. I have to admit, as much as I hated the bastard with every sinew, I was almost touched when he said he looked into my eyes. I guess even amongst devils, it's good to be seen.

"Thanks."

"Hurry the fuck up," he said and walked away, leaving me to my work. "I'll be back with a lantern."

I climbed down a short ladder and found myself in a bare brick-walled room. The floor was littered with blankets and the garbage of assorted single-serving sustenance containers. I spied nothing else until my night-vision adjusted and I turned around. A shriek of terror would have escaped if not for my hands flying to hold it prisoner.

Crumpled and folded together in the back corner of the room were two people. I blinked rapidly to be sure I was right. It had been a while since we had added new skin to our ranks, and I had truly hoped never to add more. The sight of this pair, however, ripped into my heart and nearly took me to my knees.

There was a girl of porcelain with a high forehead and sunken cheeks, eyes as big and black as paint drops on a sheet. Haggard elegance made her look barely human. She was a slip of suffering, far too good for this world. She was guarding the other, an old woman with eyes so gray and shiny they reflected the sparse light in the room like mirror shards. Her hair was a shock of frazzled gray cords on one half of her head, the other had been either eaten or scratched or burnt away by something of this hard land.

The pale girl stood with a shard of something in her hand—a piece of tin can flattened and folded to a point—but I was oddly unconcerned for myself. Her well-being was, for no discernible or logical reason, something I wanted to assure. If it had been a child...I might have done the unspeakable for the sake of mercy, ending myself in the process.

She looked into my eyes as I thought all of this, and her face went soft and pleading as she realized I meant her no harm. For the first time it perhaps an agonizingly long and lonely time, a person who meant her no harm.

She dropped her makeshift weapon and grasped onto my arms, looking deep into my eyes for the humanity she wished to find.

I looked into her frightened doe face with eyes of shimmering ink and felt every edge of me was sweating with violent, wild, impossible thought. How could I deny them this prize? Kill her right then and there? I could lie and say she was crazed. That she attacked me. They would know. I was still larger in frame and even if I spoke with every engine of my mind fueled by the illusion of veracity, they might still kick my skull into my brains just for denying them a female.

The boards groaned under the *par-ump* of booted, rolling footfalls above. I turned my sweat-slicked brow back to those wide, innocent, pleading eyes and looked deep into them, trying to communicate all I hadn't the time to say. I braced my whole body, took a breath and a gulp…and ran the point of the hook knife into her lower abdomen. Very lower.

Slender, elegant fingers curled over my forearm and I trembled under her soiled-silk touch. Resignation arose like a flood in those dark pans staring into my soul.

"Don't speak, don't move, act dumb, and do exactly as I say," I said, as seriously and clearly as I'd ever spoken a word, "if you don't want your every orifice brutalized this very night. Bite down on this and get ready."

I pulled a wad of wound-cleaning cloth from my belt and shoved it between her teeth. She closed her eyes and bit hard as I pulled the steel crescent about an inch toward her naval. She squeaked in pain.

The cut wasn't deep. I was careful about that. But the blood escaped from her in a frightening rush, washing my hands with warmth. She was nearly bones, and I couldn't avoid some muscle damage, but I hoped in equal measure to my caution that it was nothing beyond my control.

"What was that?" My master called down, followed by one of his remarkably profane names for me.

I pulled the rag from the mouth of my new and heaviest responsibility. "Found some people down here." I kept my voice low and raspy so as not to alert another pair of crusty ears. I knew my owner and his cohorts, and a dispute over ownership could mean copious amounts of blood spilled, including my own. "Two females. One's injured."

"Everyone's injured, dipshit. How bad?"

"I can stop the bleeding, but she's got a bad gash just above the pubic bone. It's up to you what you want to do, but if anyone sets on her, she'll bleed to death in seconds in her state."

"Shut ehp," he said, the side-mouth drawl bleeding through as it did when he was in thought.

"I'm just telling you—"

"*Sheht ehp*! I'll handle it. Getcher candy ass up here with our find 'less you want a hook in you tonight."

"Give me a minute," I said as though I hadn't even heard his threat. After a time, it almost sounded to my own ears like a married couple bickering.

"What about her?" the bleeding angel finally spoke. Her voice was but a whisper, but it was a Heavenly choir to my ears.

"Your mother?" I asked quickly.

"No. I found her wandering in the woods."

"I can't save her. I'm sorry." My words were callous and quick, any emotion I could summon cut from them by the urgency of my work. I was nearly finished. I would have to stitch her up later, but the flow of blood was manageable.

I expected a fight. A woman so gentle and smart would surely have the fiery strength inside to deny the abandonment of a helpless soul. Instead, I saw only sorrowful acceptance, and it was like dagger in my chest. How much had she seen already to resign to such an idea so easily? Shock dawned in her eyes, then a crest of sadness like the break of a midnight wave, then resignation as I tracked her gaze back to the blind old woman. We both knew what was to come.

"We have to get up there," I told her, plain and flat. "There will be punishment if we don't. I know it hurts, but you have to move."

With some slight aid of my lazy master, who spent more time eyeing his prize with one of his fellows than lending a hand, we were able to get them both up the ladder. I believe the old woman was mostly deaf, as well. She kept calling longingly for Charles, and my heart both broke and swelled for her. She must have missed him terribly. Husband, child, animal; whoever he was. The loneliness must have been dreadful for her tired heart to bear.

Seeing no value in her withered frame, my master drug her out of the house, dashed her head against a rotted stump, and stomped on her neck. And that was it. Her longing was no more.

I didn't even know her name.

The girl, the one I could protect for the time being, turned her head away in a teary wash. My heart broke much more for her. Right down the middle, then cracked outward from there. When I reminded the men of her condition, I met with a fist to the jaw and another to the gut, but they listened to reason. Once she healed, they could make a full meal of their brutal pleasure. Patience wasn't a virtue I should have expected in such beasts, but I was thankful for it.

A cold gust blew through, and with nothing left to scavenge, our caravan scrambled to depart. The girl, this dove with skin of milk and almond eyes, was placed into a cage and I, to my jubilation, was allowed to remain near.

We rolled up the road, into more of the cold and dark.

"How did this happen? When did people start to enjoy being so evil?" She asked me on the first night, as I stitched her wound by weak firelight in the midst of a dozen sleeping devils.

"They always enjoyed it. It was just a matter of time."

"But now is the time for kindness and hope. Now is the time for humanity to love."

"Now is the time of nothing. There is no love and no hope."

I didn't want those words to come out of my mouth

For the next weeks I tended to her dehydration and blood loss, checking her every few hours, making every excuse I possibly could to be by her side. We spoke quietly of little things, of memories both empty and full. At every turn she attempted to break through my shell, to bring out something real, something not held back and stuck away to be protected from a world so cruel. She was open, she was nurturing. She treated me as if I was a hero, complimenting my every move. Even when I informed her how to tear her stitches just a little to prolong the injury. She thought I was a godsend.

"You've given me something to believe in," she said one night while the wind howled and teeth of cold nipped every digit. I made an excuse to cover her cage with a tarp so that I could more easily change her bandages. "I was beginning to believe there wasn't any goodness left in the world. Then, just as I was praying my hardest, you showed up. I know things will be ok."

"Why are you so optimistic?" I asked. I couldn't believe how in the midst of all this...*impossibility*...she could hold onto anything but despair.

"I have hope."

"There's nothing to hope for."

"That's not true. I hoped to meet a kind person. I prayed to God that there was someone strong and kind left and I met you. Now we have each other."

"I'm not strong and there's no God in this gristle and bone."

"But I have you," she said, glimmering crescents of firelight dancing in the black of her eyes.

My throat went tight. "Yes. You have me, for the time."

"There is a God. There's hope and there is light."

"Nothing brought me to you, we were scavenging and we found you. It's as simple as that. I admire your outlook, but it's dangerous. You have to let that hope die, and if it won't die, you have to kill it."

"If you truly believe all that, why haven't you killed yourself?"

"I don't want to kill myself, just the part that's still alive. The part that feels."

"No. You're afraid, and you hold on to something inside. After all this time, you still feel. That's hope."

I looked into her face once again, fell into that beautiful stare, and denied with a terrible conviction what my heart was beginning to feel. "We are rancid grease in a pan. There is *nothing* left to hold onto in this world."

"Believe what you want to believe. I have hope. You never know what tomorrow will bring."

I could not withhold my frustration. "There hasn't been a tomorrow in a long time. Even if there was, my view on it hasn't changed. Tomorrow...is just a tragedy waiting to happen."

Her hand moved like water off slow melting ice. She caressed my face until an uncovered spring of emotion brought tears to my eyes. My skin felt as hot as embers against her icy touch, but she did not pull back.

She called me her dead-eyed angel. A darkness that shines.

That's when I knew how it would be. That's when I knew I'd protect her at all costs.

I felt love.

"That's what you should call me. Hope."

He kicked me hard and fast, creating a thumping, staccato rhythm on my chest cavity. He huffed and puffed and gossamer threads of spittle waved out from his lips as the webs of baby spiders taking flight. It wasn't from exertion, however. It was frustration and anger. I thought my chest could collapse, that my bowels might pop and flood my guts, that my spine might crack domino-style from skull to tailbone, but I knew the true power of his blows. He wasn't trying to kill me.

After the blows ceased, I heaved on the ground before my master, in the spot in the woods where he had pulled me by the collar.

"You think I don't know what you're doin'?"

"I'm sorry, master."

"No master shit right now, you soft, slimy dog prick!

"Would you like me to be your dog, sir?"

"*Shut! Up!* You think anybody—*anybody!*—is going to let you have that girl? You think I don't see you walking like you got a purpose? *She is meat!* She's gonna be stretched and pulled 'til you'll have to fold what's left like a torn, bloody rag!"

I coughed blood into the soil and breathed in the stale and fetid petrichor of the planet's carcass. "I know that."

"Then what the hell are you doing?"

"I don't know."

"Thinking you can be with her?"

"I don't know."

"Thinking that love conquers all?

"I don't know!"

"Getting your hopes up so that when she screams and begs for you to save her, you'll find the strength to be anything more than a weak, shriveled, im...imp...*impotent* pile of spineless, good-for-nothing shit?"

"*I don't know!*"

"Then maybe some hidden strength will rise up inside you? No! No! That's not the world and it never was! You'll either get hollowed out and killed with her, or the thin line bent so hard inside you will finally snap and you'll cave your own head in with a rock. Either way, I'll be eating what's left of my pet in a week or two."

"Then just do it now," I said. I was choking back tears, which made me think his abhorrence for weakness really would drive him to end my life.

"Oh...I know what this is really about. What's got hope squirmin' up in your guts. It's the one you told me about. From before the world died."

"*Noo!*" I wailed like a grief-stricken old man.

"The one that hurt ya. Yeah, it is. The one that broke ya down and left your sorry ass like roadkill. You want another chance? Is that it? Well guess what, bubba, she went on and lived a happy life without thinking of you, and she got roasted in the big fire with someone else's hard dick in her cooter and a smile on her face. It ain't comin' back. This is all that's left for you."

"*Stop, please.*"

My tears beat the earth with all the fury and sadness I had inside.

"She's gone and *you're here in Hell with me, boy!*"

The look on his face when I sprang from the ground and launched a fist at his gut was something I never thought I'd see. My knuckles hit cotton-wrapped rock and my wrist buckled, but I drove into him, pushing and crying until he snatched me up like a child, tossed me against a tree, and I heard the gentle hissing cry of freedom of a blade loosed from its sheath.

The edge pressed to my throat, cold and hot at the same time, and foul breath of garbage and decay belched like a blast furnace in my face. His eyes were wide and yellow and full of sober rage like I'd never seen. I thought then I was dead, and I felt thankful and relieved. I wanted it to finally be over, but I was also afraid. And that perturbed me.

"That's something I never thought I'd see outta you," was all he said. We huffed ragged breath into one another's faces while he searched my eyes for something I could not discern. "There might just be some rocks in your sack, after all. You tend to 'em, let 'em grow. There better be somethin' hard in you for what's to come. I'll let you carry on with her, so long's you remember. She's already dead. Ain't nothin' you can do to save her. When the time comes, you're gonna end her yourself, to save her from any more pain. That'll be the final act. You'll be just another monster in this world then."

When we returned to our nightly camp, she knew I had been beaten. I had to signal her to remember what I said. Do not show concern or attachment to me. It would be used against us for sadistic fun.

Later, when the goblins were asleep, she held me, rubbing my tender bruises with fingers anointed in tears.

I realized then that I had to do something. Feelings such as I had discovered leaking from me were highly dangerous. Letting a person get so close to a heart is absolutely nothing but risk, I knew that from so long ago. Never let anyone too close. In the old days they'd use you, hurt you, and leave you. In the new days, they'd just get you killed.

I blurted so suddenly I was surprised it emerged as more than incoherent pus. "I'm going to get us out of here."

My whole body shook with fear, but the look in her eyes was worth the threat of a barbaric death by immolation. "I will," I asserted, staring into two peaceful pools of oil black. She was questioning me already, begging me with her face not to get hurt. Her immediate attachment to me forged an inner armor. I had wanted to help so many people, even tricked myself into believing that I nursed the diseased mutants to whom we belonged because it was my nature when the truth was I wished I had the power to slaughter them all.

But Hope...I wanted to save. If anything in the blasted hellscape of my life was worth dying for...it was her. For the first time, I was unafraid for myself.

I finished tending to her as was my routing and returned to my shelter. My master, still high and excited from hurting me, wanted to show his affection. Violence was the world's last drug, and he was a junkie of magnitude.

I took it, perhaps for the first time, like a man. Not the man that went limp and cried into the dust as my body bucked forward, skimming my face across the ground like so many cold nights, but a man with resolve and anger in his heart. My master noticed this and took it as a challenge, he put more of his already spent reserves into trying to make me cry out. I did not.

When it was over, Skullfucker stood up, hiking his pants. "I see it in your face. You're almost ready to kill."

"I'll never be like you," I said, holding myself tightly.

"Sure ya will, you spineless little shit-mound. It's why you're still alive and not another skull I've split open and shot my rocks in. You're gonna be my main bitch, and you're gonna be a tough little whore. You keep oozin' tears and snot like a diseased cunt flap if you want to end up in the pot, though. Your choice."

"You need me."

He turned and kicked me in the ribs until I balled up tight in agony. "Don't need nothin' no more, you dumb scrote sucker! The world's dead! You think anyone cares about you because you're a soft little dandelion that patches a scratch here and there? You either stand up straight when you walk out of this tent with me in the morn' or be ready to fill some bellies. That's all there is to it. I'll be back soon to get some sleep. Don't fuckin' try to hold me tonight. I don't want the stench of your weakness on me."

He left me in my roly-poly ball of endless misery. Hopelessness spiraling down to the depths of my soul. I cried cold, heavy tears that hit the earth at my face like beads of glass. After a time, my mind shut down as it so often did to keep itself alive. Numbness washed over me as I let my body fall open with a plan forming in the image before my eyes.

My master's belt lie on the ground beside his mat, with his wicked knives sleeping in their sheaths.

I realized then the cruelest thing he wished to do to me. He hadn't kept me alive for the value of my skills or the ease of my compliance. It wasn't any hidden affection or vision of worth. He kept me alive to see if he could make someone like me into someone like him. That would be his most vicious kick. Peeling back all of me that was gentle to reveal the flower of decay inside.

He was drunk on perhaps the last vodka the world would ever taste when his strong but wobbly body stumbled in and fell almost instantly to sleep. When I wrenched open his throat with the mightiest thrust my arms could obey, the foul smell of that wretched mix in his stomach nearly made me vomit into him.

I lied on his body with my full weight, breathing hard with the exertion of holding him down, forcing the blade into the ground beneath his neck until he stopped kicking. When the final spasms rolled through and the last rattle in his lungs gurgled bubbles of blood onto my face, I took from him what there was of any value to me, covered his body and kicked dirt over the bloody pool seeping into the earth. I didn't need keys for any shackles. We didn't need them. It was known by all of the enslaved that running meant a fate worse than death, before the gift of death finally fell upon the. No one ran, no one escaped.

That was the night it all changed.

We slipped away into the grave of the world. All quiet, all dark. Only the glow of the clouds overhead gave any light by which to navigate a path of no direction. Even the moon was dead.

All I carried was a lantern and the knife of my dead master. She was healed enough to limp along quickly without an abundance of pain, and once we were far enough down a dirt road I bade her to run. Tearing her stitches or further aggravating the wound were the least of our worries. We were lost in a world without geography, frightened and cold in the dark. We were a scream away from ruin. The sweat rolling down my back froze in the dreaded sundown of panic.

"Where are we going?"

"I don't know."

She squeezed my hand. "I trust you."

"But I don't know!"

"You will."

What was left of the sun behind the ashen heap of dust called a sky would turn the world from black to gray in a few hours. I led her down a side path into the frightening woods. I prayed that whatever might lie ahead of us, if anything, would kill us faster than what lie behind.

Her grip tightened with sudden ferocity, which stopped me cold, and as I followed her startled stare to find that we had wound our way to the edge of a great pit in the ground. Not a drop off or precipice, but something dug at some point in time. My guess; a mass grave.

She looked into my eyes and kissed me. "We could just jump. I see you're afraid, but I'm not. Say the word and we don't have to run anymore. I know we have nowhere to go. No food or water. I'm so sorry I took you away. You gave up your only life to save me."

"You saved *me*." It was a croak of brutal honesty and love. "Don't talk like that. Let's go."

We trudged away from the pit, up the path to a clearing where the remnants of a camp and the bones of its settlers remained. I pulled the tattered tarp-cloth of their once-shelter to the base of a tree and we collapsed on our marital bed. Her breathing was slow but labored, and it plucked at the strings of my fear.

We held each other close until she grew tired curled up catlike against my legs, her head in my lap. She traced circles around my knee as if it were a fresh wound.

"What do you think is the most important thing is life?"

I ran my hands through her grimy hair. "I honestly don't know. Truth to oneself, I suppose. If you don't keep that, you're just a picture of someone that looks like you."

"I never understood how some people are able to hide who they are inside. Put on masks and pretend to be strong when they're not, or lie through their teeth, or just be cruel even though we all hurt sometimes. Or maybe we should all be monsters like… them. Maybe we should just be evil and not feel anything."

"You think those men don't feel? They're not devil's born for this world. They're as broken and lost and terrified as you and I. They're shaking and gnashing in the maw of the end, and when it comes they hope it will be quick and violent, but when it isn't, they'll cry and scream and thrash and grip onto whatever's left alive to cry on as they slip into the void."

"Then they should show it. No one is so irredeemable they can't be loved. You just have to open up.

"It's a sentiment that didn't even work in the old world. No one showed the raw meat inside. People just don't accept it."

"I do. I've only ever wanted to just be how I feel. Maybe I just wasn't made for the world."

Of course she wasn't. She was something kind and compassionate. Such a being had no place outside of the realm of dreams.

"Why did you try to save the old woman? Why not just end it quickly?"

"Because that's not me. I've always tried to save things. I was neglected by my parents. I grew up in a place with no love, maybe that's why I was always reaching out to save things. So I could love them. I look for the light inside of people. I want to keep it burning."

"A romantic. One of the most dangerous things to be if you can't control it."

"When I was a child, I rescued a bird from a neighborhood cat. I took it home, tried to feed it, but it was badly injured. I knew my father would kill it, so I left it in the barn overnight. I thought it might just freeze to death, but when I checked on it the next morning I saw the rats had gotten it. I was devastated. I had nightmares for weeks about how it was slowly toyed with and eaten. It was my fault. I caused that pain by trying to save it."

"You didn't know. You did what you could and tried to protect it from harm. That's a pretty wonderful thing."

"It didn't feel wonderful. It seems like so much I tried to help, I just ended up hurting more. Have you ever felt pain and love for something so strongly you just want to protect it from everything?"

"Yes," I said softly, the chain of sudden emotion tightening around my neck. "I want to tell you a story. Of a man I knew before all of this."

"Yes, please," she said, her mind beginning to dream as her eyes hung open.

"He was a patient in my care. Very kind, very gentle. I was very lonely then and we became friends very quickly."

"It hurts me to think of you lonely."

"His stories…his life. He'd seen so much tragedy and suffering. The things he had gone through made me weep at night. A childhood without hope, difficulties with everything, a life where the future always seemed like a fake carrot on the end of a cruel stick. He had loved just once. A single love in all those years, and he had lost her. He had a broken heart that never healed. I wondered how a person so beaten, so crushed by disappointment had endured. A life unrealized isn't a life. It's just waiting for the day you die. He kept saying that there is always hope, that you never know what tomorrow might bring. Each day he persisted through suffering and sadness, knowing that nothing would get better but saying with tears in his eyes that it just might. He said that focusing on the sad things in life is just…weaving melancholies."

"I like that," she whispered. "So much sadness, like a web between the stars that we're all caught in…the whole planet."

"He became my best friend. I came to care for him so deeply I couldn't bear to see him suffer like that anymore. His body was degrading slowly but his mind was sharp, and he remembered so much. If he'd been fading in his head, it would have been different. But he was a prisoner. A broken man looking back on a life of sadness."

"What happened?"

"I went in one day and told him I had good news. I calmed him, stroked his head—like I'm doing to you now—and looked into his eyes while I administered the dose that sent him off to sleep. No more suffering, no more heartache. Just peace. He didn't know it was coming. I told him to sleep, and that I had great news. That tomorrow, everything was going to be better. He smiled before he closed his eyes...and that was that."

"I'm so sorry," she said, tears rolling onto my lap. She ground her forehead against me, mewling as the very thought rendered her tremulous. "You were so strong to do something like that. You must have been so sad. I can't stand the thought of you sad. I love you so much. So much I can't let you feel sadness or anything bad."

"I was only sad before. Only before. It took everything I had to keep him from seeing me cry, but when he was gone, for a moment all I felt was relief. After that was a loneliness so fierce my whole body trembled. I sat before him and wept. I had to carry his memories, his stories, his pain. Where he had been there was just nothing, and it caused me ceaseless agony every day. But I carried it for him. I felt better knowing he was free. He was no longer a victim."

My tears fell into her hair.

"I'm so sorry I did this to you. We shouldn't have left. You're a savior, a healer. You had a purpose. I should've just accepted what I was meant for. I've always been a victim."

"No more," I said. "That all ends now. We won't be anyone's victims ever again."

She climbed my body until we stared into one another's eyes. "You have my whole heart and soul. If you should fall from here, I will carry you. I will fight wherever we go to protect you, and your heart will never ache of loneliness ever again. I love you," she said.

"And I love you. I didn't think I could feel anything again but fear and disgust. But against every odd, I found you. Even if we go to some dark, cold place to wait for death, I will protect you and hold you. I love you with all of me."

"Then kiss me. Hold me. Make love to me now."

"You're   hurt."

"I'm okay. Just love me and fall asleep with me and if we don't wake up, I'll drift off happily in your arms. Say you're mine."

"I'm yours."

"And I'm yours. Kiss me, please, and don't stop."

I kissed her.

Now I sit in the light of morning's embers, reeling on the edge of an impossible wish. I almost wish I hadn't met her. I had only felt such pain and loss twice before, and both times it nearly drove me to end myself. I imagine how well taken care of she could've been by someone stronger. If someone had her, wouldn't they cherish something so rare and delicate? I've always taken care of my things, but only so long as my things weren't taken.

Even in this gangrenous fester of a world, I can't image most know what it's like to survive as I have. I've never been strong, or sturdy, or firm. I've never been good enough at anything to warrant much use. In my days I've cried, covered in snot and mud, pleaded for what little mercy might be given. I've been a bitch to large, rough men. Been a handmaiden and servant to whichever gangs would take me for my paltry offerings. I've been bartered and sold as meat, made to dance with my genitals tucked between my legs for the amusement of sadistic brigands who laughed and whooped and pelted me with rocks and food, who would threaten to slit my throat if I cast so much as a hateful eye.

This world is custom-tailored hell for one such as me, and still I am in it.

It is done. I feel easier knowing she'll be no one's toy as I have been.

She was bleeding again after we loved. With the caring blanket of a few soft whispers, she drifted into a deep sleep. She would not live long in her weakened state unless we returned to camp.

I could not save her and I could not protect her.

I did it with my old master's knife, through the back of the neck. I held her down, and calmed her the best I could while her body moved in those few terrible moments. "I'm sorry, I'm sorry,"

I said over and over. "They can't hurt you now. I love you so much."

I don't believe she fully woke up, which comforts me to no end. It was the hardest and most important thing I've ever had to do. A sacrifice so great I wanted to be the one to die, but that same terrible fear now stills my hand.

At dawn, I wrapped her body in the bloodstained tarp with the greatest of care, as if she were a dove of my very own, then slowly, crying tears of awful joy, I drug her back along our trail and rolled her body into the pit.

The suffering within me was cavernous, immeasurable, but as the body I would never touch again fell into shadows I felt a sense of calm and relief. I let go.

Hope is the jagged rock to which all souls cling. The rope around our necks that keeps us dangling above the abyss. Hope keeps us going when even fear is not enough. That terrible curse of hope is the light that promises and leads us through the dark times, and now my hope lies at the bottom of that pit.

There is only mud, and darkness, and death.

But my love and my heart is free. She is safe and eternal.

I leave the forest for a future unknown. Should I encounter those I fled, I will fight to free what prisoners remain. I will kill whom I can and die if I must. And if I survive, I will take what is mine from the dead and find a new place in whatever time I have left in this umbra.

Suffering is a sword I carry inside. I see her face when I close my eyes. She is with my friends and my family, and they are not smiling, not laughing. They are rotting.

I see dim fire in the distance, and an icy breeze freezes the tears on my face.

I smell the scent of blood in the air.

I can't help the thoughts crawling like spiders in the back of my brain. I see myself bringing her to the loving end. I did it with all the tenderness and mercy in my heart, yet with delirious terror I don't understand, I cannot deny how much I enjoyed it.

Hearts in the Dark

Asiatic lilies, he told the corner florist on the street just before the canal.

"Lucky lady," the little woman said with a chuckle. Her back was curved like a reed bent by the winds of time, but her eyes shone with startling ferocity. At first, he was unsure if the comment was snide or sincere, but quickly decided that worry was a weight far too plentiful to be gathered at every occasion.

"Lucky me," he said with more mirth than any time in his life. The smile on his face, though slight and restrained, was the widest that had ever pried his lips.

"A lad in love. Good for you, sonny."

He was in love, and it was good.

His name was Peter. He had met Lily on the night of his thirtieth birthday, and could still picture in stark relief the night he first laid eyes on her.

She had asked, "Do I look like a monster?"

He was sitting alone in the park, watching the rippled water cast monstrous translations back at him through broken reflections, contemplating the fearful thought of another thirty years of existence.

When her words met his ears he had no response. Captivated, he could only stare at this pale creature glowing like candle wax in the moonlight.

"No," he had said at last. "Do I?"

Then she turned and ran, and he had risen to ask if she needed help, but her movements were frighteningly quick and he was not keen to chase a lone and obviously troubled woman. It could have been any meaningless encounter, one of a hundred million ants brushing antenna across his life in a millisecond's collapse before disappearing into the night. But this one stuck like a punch to the gut, like it was supposed to mean something. Something he could not understand.

He headed for home, alone and somber in the cool breeze of the night. The long way around sounded good, as it so often did. It would take him by the bridge where old thoughts came calling from the water like soggy phantoms from long submerged dreams. Demons sing in such sweet voices, and everyone loves a lullaby.

It was on the Cranston Bridge, where he walked often trying to summon the courage to do what she herself was attempting that very moment. She was even in his chosen spot, draped in a heavy black overcoat, with swatches of blood across her hands and face.

If not for his continual thoughts of that location, he very well could have missed her entirely.

Suddenly concerned, he hopped the interior balustrade and approached. Was she bleeding? Had he missed noticing the blood on her face in the park? He couldn't remember, but it was of little importance in that moment.

That moment when he could not stand to see another do with courage what had eluded him for so long.

"Please don't!"

"Why not?" she cried.

At that time—of all times!—he found no words to speak. Every trite feel-good or bullshit affirmation of life clung to his throat like dry bread, refusing to shake free. He stared, confounded at his own silence, for so long that she laughed. A sort of snappy chortle through her tears.

"You want me to not jump and you can't even give a reason why?"

Finally, a measure of thought broke free. "I come here all the time, thinking about jumping. From that exact spot, in fact. In all the times, I've only ever tried to talk myself into going through with it. Being on the other side like this...I don't know what to say."

"You've wanted to jump?" she asked, as if the very notion that didn't want to live was a perplexing puzzle. "Why?"

"Does it matter?" he stammered. "This is about you, not me."

"I want to know. Why do you want to die?"

He started on wobbly legs, throwing awful thoughts together and hoping that whatever came out, no matter how strange, would keep her from taking that fateful step. "It's not that I want to die. I'm terrified of dying. It's that I never wanted to exist. I don't...I don't even feel alive. What everyone else calls life feels like this vast sucking hole of disappointment and despair. I don't know how so many people get up in the morning. I don't know how *I* get up in the morning, but I feel like my strength is running out and I don't know what's going to happen to me."

"But...you must have good days."

"I have *okay* days. But I want best days. I don't know what a *good* day is. The best thing about yesterday is that it's gone, and the only good thing about tomorrow is that it won't be today. I just don't think my days are ever going to get any better."

"Well that's a shitty reason," she stated bluntly. "To take what life has given you and hate it like that. Not like me. What I am," she lowered her eyes to the frigid, black waters below, "what I've done. I may not look like a monster, but I am one. I'm cursed."

"You might think it's shitty," he said, inching closer to her position, "but I don't see myself much different. To think there are so many people in the world so much worse off than I am. I don't care. The world seems like it's falling apart around us some days, and I don't care. People say people like me are worthless ingrate babies, that I'm part of the problem, and I *don't fucking care*! Doesn't that sound like a monster to you? Doesn't that sound like a curse?"

"No, it sounds like you don't know what a curse really is."

"Maybe I don't, so why don't you tell me. You seem to have an awful lot to throw at me, so let's hear your perfectly justifiable reason."

"You wouldn't understand," she said, her weak voice trailing off under the wind and the growing agitation of the river. Her bare feet slid to the edge. "It's better this way."

That moment, he panicked and pounced, leaping onto the outer balustrade right beside her. "Then take me with you!"

At a closer glimpse he saw that her face, even gaunt and drawn by sadness and surprise, was lovely. Her eyes, even clouded with despair, shed vibrant waves of luminescence.

"What are you doing? Get down!"

"No!"

"Why are you here?" she shouted in his face.

"Because you need me to be! Because when I saw you in the park I know that it meant something, because even though I'm tired and I'm hungry and it's my fucking birthday, I chose tonight to come here. That meant something. And I found you standing here, ready to jump just as I wish I could do, and this *means something!*"

"It's your birthday?" she asked, wiping away the remnants of tears largely abated by umbrage.

"Unfortunately, yes. And I don't care if it's my last. But I honestly don't think it's the same for you. Get down with me and I'll take you anywhere you want to go."

"I don't have anywhere."

"Then I'll stay with you. As long as you want or need. I promise."

Now it was her turn to be struck dumb, and without even realizing it was happening, she let him coax her down from the ledge.

"You would do that for me?" she said when they were away from the ledge. She pulled the coat tighter against the chill.

"If it's what you want. If it will help. Like I said, it's not like I'm that worried about myself. I just want you to feel better."

"Why? I'm nobody to you."

"You're someone enough. Because we have something in common. Because I admire your courage. And because, well, I don't really know what else. Let's just take things as they come, and I'll think of more reasons later."

This brought the smallest, most hopeful bit of laughter. The tears had largely dried to clear, clean trails down her face. "I'm sorry."

"About what?"

"About the things I said to you. About you. I was upset and I didn't mean it like that." Without thinking, without regard for convention or familiarity, she leaned into him.

"It's okay," he said. "It's okay."

When she left the bridge with him that night, it was as though she had, in a few short moments, become a different person. And his promise was kept. They walked together a long time that night, through the areas of the city that were brightly lit, staying close in a way that, to him, was both surprising and exciting. They stopped only once for her to wash her face at a fountain, and she gave barely a whisper about what had led them to meet. He never asked her about the blood, the oversized coat, or why she was so uneasy. If there was trouble in her life, it was all he could do to make her feel like she had somewhere safe with him, if she desired.

Finally, near a women's shelter, she tried to flee him and he promised not to follow on one condition that he wouldn't enforce anyway, but nevertheless hoped desperately that she could comply.

"Meet me here tomorrow night. Please."

"Why? You don't know me, and you already did your good deed. Why do you want to see me again?"

"I'm done thinking of why for the night," he said immediately. "I don't need to know why you were in the park, or on the bridge, or what you're running from. I didn't ask why, so please don't ask me now."

"You can't rescue me. Not the way you think."

"And you can't rescue me. I just want to see you again."

For a moment she wavered, hesitating. "You don't even know my name?"

"I'd love to know it, if you want to tell me."

She looked back with eyes that seemed as though they were seeing something for the first time. Perhaps they were truly seeing him. "Okay," she agreed at last. "Tomorrow night. And it's Lily."

She hurried on after that, and when she thought he couldn't see, she dashed past the shelter and down an alley.

Every bit of him wanted to give chase, but he steadied himself and turned away, hoping that if faith and trust had brought her with him off that bridge, it would return them together once again.

It did.

She met him just as they agreed, shed of the oversized coat. This time she wore a dress with stray threads here and there, obviously secondhand. It was then he figured for certain she must have been homeless, and though every instinct ordered him to offer her his apartment, he restrained himself as he said he would, relenting that it was not his job nor desire to rescue her. Despite the penury of her appearance, her very presence was fair and dignified. Her eyes were pellucid, the color of bluebells in the morning light.

But, as it turned out, they rescued each other. The next several weeks were a flurry of snapshots, each slightly more intimate than the last, as they came to know and care for one another. Worries, fears, struggles; all flew from their lips as if being cast off like iron chains, no longer able to dash or demoralize their hopes. Soon, what hopes they had were shared, melded further into a future dream with every whisper, caress, and embrace.

The only thing he worried about was the presence of what seemed to be sickness. She was frequently pallid and at times lethargic, with a phlegmy cough that appeared sporadically. Every time he broached the subject of medical care, he was shut down firmly but with gentle grace. There was an essence in there that he admired, that coexistence of independence and softness of spirit. The world all too often turned people into brittle, jagged things. Her edges were hard but smooth to the touch.

It happened like a slow drip of oil from a bottle until finally all resistance and worry had drained, and what remained was a pure exhilaration that in his deepest heart, he called love.

Slightly further along the stream of time, that love found them together when, for the first of hopefully many occasions, she agreed to return with him to his apartment. There was a kind of sad elation when she accepted his earnest offer. It was an anxious step that would allow them a deeper privacy and the comfort to grow closer, but he dismayed at what mundanity he had to offer.

"It's beautiful," she said, taking in the simple comfort of his modest abode.

"You're too kind. It's a plain box, but it's home."

"You have a nice touch," she assured him.

"It's a clumsy touch."

She smiled. "Not with me."

There was wine, which he was as reluctant to offer as she was to ask, and in the end they opted for water and gentle music, and the chance to speak in dulcet tones. The simple drink was but a placebo for their nerves, the notes an odd emulsifier for smooth conversation. And so they revealed, as far as two people can, themselves each to the other—

"You ever wonder why we're here? If love—"

"Go on."

"Never mind. I'm just being boring."

"You're never boring to me. And love certainly isn't boring."

"But it is painful."

"It can be."

—until along some time in the evening a knock at the door flew Peter into a near panic.

"What is it?" she asked with a measure of alarm that could not nearly equal his own.

"Open up, Vance," a muffled voice called through the door.

"You have to hide."

"I have to *what*?"

"Please!" He entreated, as if fearful for her safety. "Just in the bedroom. It's a guy from work. He," his eyes darted back and forth, shuffling between truth and lie, "he gives me a hard time. I don't want him to see you here."

In what he found to be her astounding capacity for acceptance, she nodded and allowed him to guide her to the bedroom, where he closed the door, and quickly erased any indicator of her presence.

"I said open the door," the voice came again with authority.

When Peter opened the door, he was greeted by the shoulder of a taller, sandy haired man with a sharp nose and a complexion that screamed self-tan.

"Evening, Nigel," Peter said as the man pushed past him into the apartment. "Won't you come in?"

"You did good today, Pete." Nigel Porter said as he scanned the room with derision. "Backing me up like that. Have to say, I appreciate it."

"No problem," Peter feigned. "Whatever helps a co-worker. Maybe it'll lead to that promotion everyone's after."

"Maybe," Nigel said, but it was long and drawn out, dripping with the exaggeration of doubt. *Just maybe, Pete ol' boy. Maaaaaaaaaybeeeee.* "But you know what I think would really clench it?"

"I'm sure you're going to tell me."

The next words turned Peter's blood cold. "If you withdrew your name."

Suddenly struggling to spit out the words, Peter dropped his folded arms in a defeat of sorts. "How did you find out?"

"You don't have to worry about the fine details, little buddy. Nice place, by the way." Nigel's forehead was high and tended to shine, but now it reflected light like a greased pig's ass, as if he were oozing some oleaginous essence to make himself even more unpleasant. "Let's just talk about how you're going to help me next, how about that?"

"Nigel, I'm not going to pull—"

"Oh yes, you are," he said, that reflective oil running down to his mile-wide grin.

If a snake could smile, Peter thought.

Nigel continued, "Because I can do more to help both of us from that position than you could ever help yourself. I can be a good friend, Pete. Or...if you'd rather be an ungrateful little snot-nose."

"Nige, look," Peter began.

"*What* did you say?"

Lily watched the odd and intense confab through a crack in the door no wider than a pencil. She did not like the man named Nigel from the onset, but the moment Peter uttered the name *Nige* there was a palpable alteration in the air. She feared aggression was on tap for the evening.

"Nigel, sorry."

"You bet your ass, you are."

"I don't think it's right for you to come in here, into my apartment, and start telling me that I—"

"Your *apartment?*" Nigel said with a chuckle. "You think these walls offer you some protection from me, Petey boy?" The taller man slapped his hands on Peter's shoulders like a football coach about to dish out some motivation. "How thick are these walls, you think?"

Peter didn't answer, but watched Nigel's oily face and simmering eyes exude a dreadful threat of violence.

"Pete, Pete. You're making this far too complicated. Messy, even." He leaned in close, blitzing Peter with a puff of breath and reeked of onions cooked in peppermint oil. "It doesn't have to be. So let's try this one...last...time. What are you going to do for your old pal tomorrow?"

Peter was silent for several long seconds. To Lily, waiting as stiff and quiet as a dead mouse down the hall, it was like a rubber band being stretched toward her eyes. The intensity of waiting for it to snap would break her resolve if the silence was not broken first.

"I'm going to withdraw my name," Peter said finally, a forlorn look of defeat weighing his eyes to the floor.

"That's a good chap. Don't worry, you won't regret it."

Just when Lily thought she was free to breathe comfortably, there was a soft *whoomp*! like a heavy head hitting a freshly puffed pillow, and Peter went to his knees on the hardwood.

"You just don't ever make me wait like that again. Just consider this a lesson is respect. I'll be your boss soon, after all."

All of the preceding events Lily had watched with a sense of mounting anxiety blooming into panic with each silent tick of time crashing through the still air. That is, until Peter plummeted to his knees, whereupon her immediate panic was suddenly engulfed by an all-burning desire to see him righted. The strength of this emotional tide nearly took the breath that was floating stagnate in her lungs. She worried and wondered. How could she have fallen in love with a man whom she had known so briefly? Was it his willingly open heart, his intense kindness, or merely a poignant yearning evoked from the chasm of loneliness deep within. The truth was as unpleasant as entrails in a box, and not one she wished to unpack.

I love him, she thought.

"Take care, little buddy," Nigel said, and no sooner was he down the hall than Lily was at Peter's side, comforting with tender hands and loving words.

"Are you okay? Are you hurt?

"Just a bruised ego. I'm fine."

"Who *was* that?"

"A guy from the company. Don't worry about him. He's upset because his fists hit harder than his wit."

"Oh, sweetheart, please get up."

His eyes sprayed radiant light as staggeringly bright as the first break of day on the horizon. "You called me sweetheart."

"I suppose I did. Now please get up."

With her aid, Peter climbed to his feet and slapped the invisible dust of damaged pride from his slacks. "Is it bad that I wish he would disappear next?"

He couldn't read the look that filled her face, but an instant of fear clenched his heart, as if he had said some terrible thing about a newborn child.

"You...you really shouldn't talk like that. I understand, but—"

"No, I'm sorry," he said quickly.

"My God, the time! I have to go."

"What? Why?"

"I just—I have to. I can't stay any longer, I'm sorry."

"What? Why?"

"I'm sorry," she said, heading quickly for the door.

"But—wait! It's dangerous! What about—" he wanted to tell her it wasn't safe, late at night with the disappearances continuing to mount, but before he could utter another plea she was out the door, floating like a distressed phantom down the hall.

All of that had changed, for their love had so grown that on that night that Peter strolled with helium in his heels along the canal, he was celebrating more than just an anniversary of sorts.

He had a feeling it was going to be a wonderful night.

By the time he arrived, she was already there and the dinner table was set. The key to his apartment he had gifted to her lay on the table beside the door.

"Hello lovely."

"Evening darling."

Loving embraces punctuated their reunions now. Gone were many of the inhibitions of their early courtship. If anything, he had only further come to accept her eccentricities as endearments rather than walls between them. Her hesitance to explore each other intimately, her often times ravenous appetite, and a dismayingly early curfew only served to further ensconce his desire to know her.

They ate to music and conversed idly between sips of wine, paying no attention to the lazy flow of time that took the evening from them like a rapid stream lifting sediment from a riverbed. With only the best intentions, he made every attempt to keep her entertained and distracted. She was like a child in some respects, discovering the world for the first time in an adult body. Where others would see oddity, he saw a splendid innocence, something to be cherished and preserved.

But, like all so many well laid plans, the time arrived when she knew what he was doing, and looked back from the clock in fear. "Peter! The time!"

"I know," he said in exasperation. "Can't you stay? Just for tonight?"

"You know I can't," she said, rising quickly. "You said you would always accept even if you don't understand."

"I will. I do."

"Then accept that I have to leave."

He made no move to block her way, though his body ached to throw itself at her feet and plead for her company. "I wish you wouldn't."

"We wish all sorts of things."

"Yes, but I really, *truly* wish you didn't have to go. Won't you please just sit for a moment, until...I'm feeling better?"

"Why? What's wrong?"

"I just get the most awful feeling when you leave. I ache for more time with you."

"You're sweet."

"Not sweet enough."

The thought of him in pain swayed her resolve, and he felt immediately dirty for resorting to such measures. Then she looked at him with such deep, sorrowful eyes that all guilt was washed away by a powerful wave.

"I shouldn't," she said, head swiveling between the door and his pleading eyes.

He gestured toward the couch, "We can just sit. We don't even have to talk. Just us in the silence for a few last minutes. That's all. Please, I wouldn't ask if I didn't want you here desperately."

He couldn't know that her core was screaming to leave, that bells of panic rung in her mind, clanging a cavalcade of warning. Still, her thoughts felt unlike her own. She felt a deeper desire, one that overruled the voice telling her to leave. A desire to not be alone. "Just a few moments."

He sat down in the welcoming corner and she moved to his side. So close, closer than they had ever been. To his surprise she leaned into him, allowing his body to cradle her gently as she slumped further down into his welcome warmth.

"This is...nice," she breathed.

He saw that her eyes were closed in pleasure. "Yes," he said, "it is."

The last thing that ran through his head was an instant of happiness like a bloom of soft, warm light when her voice drifted into his ears that were half-clogged by the cottony depth of sleep.

"I'm glad I didn't jump, but I think I've fallen…"

The passage of time had no meaning for them in that space. It was a warm, quiet paradise of rest until Peter opened his eyes. It happened like waking from a long and vivid dream, as if born into a no longer familiar world, groggy and oddly confused as to one's true time and location. He was conscious only of a strange weight on his chest and something hard and slick like wet glass beneath his fingers. He began to yawn, looked down to see his sleeping beloved…and instantly felt that he had awakened in the most wretched depths of Hell.

The thing that lay upon his chest was not Lily—was not human! His heart—threatened by a surge of terror as wide as a starless night—shot to a gallop, punishing his veins with coursing blood gone ice cold.

"Oh my *God*!" he choked, a hoarse, stilted flow of terror from his pinched throat.

The thing stirred, issuing a slimy, bubbly report like a whisper through mud. "Hmm, sweetheart?"

He sprang up, pushing the hideous thing from his body and wiping furiously at the film sticking to his sweater. There was a harsh, feculent feeling upon his hands not unlike the grab of adhesive from duct tape left in the sun.

The thing shrieked and stood up on legs that were human, but were not—*could not* be Lily's. It shivered and wobbled perilously on legs that seemed too thin for its frame. It then raised its oddly jointed hands and looked at them in a way that Peter could not venture to describe.

Not her! His mind shrieked in endless cycles. *It's not Lily! Not Lily! Not Lily!*

In place of her gentle skin there was now a glabrous carapace, marked by flecks of silver and green and draped in an unctuous sheen that shone with variegated light. Bulbous, protuberant eyes jutted at him from a skull not insectoid but not fully human, a thing of nightmares.

It has to be a nightmare! His mind gibbered. *A bizarre dream! It has to be! I'll wake up and she'll be in my arms aga—*

He tumbled over the couch arm mid-thought, landing painfully on his shoulder before scrabbling onto his back, frantically kicking away from the revolting form lumbering ever closer.

"Sweetie!" the creature scream-whined, some high pitched squeal that sounded like a pig choking on a squeezebox. *"It's meeeee!"*

The cacophonous shriek chased him down the hall *"I'm sorryyyyyyy!"*

He battled for purchase on the hardwood to the *click-scrape* of his shoes like a cartoon crab in roller skates, limbs flailing helplessly as he tried to surge backward, away from the foul bugstrosity lumbering towards him with wobbly, terrifying steps.

"God no!" he screamed, as if the sound might jar him from the nightmare to awake in a trembling mess with the hand of his beloved Lily resting on his chest.

The creature was nearly over him, a near perfect distance to pin its dripping mandibles on his chest if it fell, when he was finally able to secure one heel and spring knocking one knee against the floor hard enough to rattle the lampshade beside the couch. Skirting the coffee table, narrowly avoided the obstacle that would have no doubt put him once again on the floor, he tore down the hallway as the staccato treading of the horrible creature changed direction to follow him.

"*Baaabbbyyy!*"

He clamped both hands over his ears, wanting only to shut out that terrible, pitchy drone. He covered the length of the hallway in three great strides and barreled into the bathroom at the end of the hall, closing the door with a teeth-chattering slam and locking himself therein. The panic that flooded his system was cut by a moment of sober terror when he realized that he was now trapped. Why had he not chosen the bedroom, at the very least? At his bedside was a cedar nightstand, and resting within its top drawer was a pistol that he dearly wished was in his hands.

Why? Why didn't you go for it you idiot?

Because in his deepest heart he knew. The knowledge was ugly and hard but undeniable. The legs, the words...the thing shambling down the hallway most likely looking to chew threw the door to get to him was his light and his love. That freakish being *was* Lily.

No sooner had the thought penetrated the veil of denial than the first crash upon the door sent his back to the wall. Eyes closed, he prayed to all and to nothing that he would still wake up from that insectoid nightmare.

"*Peter!*" it screeched. On the other side, there was an odd, rhythmic ticking which reminded Peter of June beetles crashing against a window on hot summer nights. "*It's me! I'm so sorry.*"

"What the...*what the hell?*" he finally blurted out, fear fracturing his voice like the chisel of puberty. "What are you?" His palms crashed into his eyes, seeking to obliterate the sleep still hanging on their lids with friction. "Oh God! Tell me I'm asleep! Tell me this is a nightmare!"

When next her voice came drifting through the door, it was no longer the harsh cry of a bug mimicking a human. It was Lily's voice, heavy the sadness the likes of which he hadn't heard since the night they met. Peter couldn't be sure if it was by her will or his own, as if by some sheer force of desire he was able to hear her voice whereas in reality she was still emitting that pitchy, undulating shrill.

"It started a few years ago. I started, changing. I thought I was going insane, thought I would hurt someone. One night, my mom was yelling at me." Her voice broke with sadness. "Screaming, throwing things. She did that sometimes when Daddy didn't come home. I couldn't control it, and I started to change in front of her. I had to run. You don't understand this hunger that was inside, how difficult it was to keep my mind from being taken over. It's indescribable."

Peter lowered his hands from his face, questions blowing like a gale wind through his mind. "How...how did it happen?"

A thump from outside, her forehead against the door. "I wish I knew. It just...happened. I've spent a lot of evenings in libraries, looking for anything that could explain it. *I don't know what I am!*" She stopped to sob uncontrollably. "I'm just cursed. I can't stay like this for long. At times, it's taken a lot to hold myself, but with you it's a little easier somehow. It's a little like flexing a muscle, and when I'm with you it's almost like I don't concentrate on it as much. That's why I lost track of time. I feel so comfortable with you. So cared for. You make me feel loved. But I change late at night. No matter how hard I try, I can't stop it. So now you know why I've been running. Now you know...why I was on the bridge that night."

It dawned on him with horrific clarity. "The blood, the disappearances. Lily, I—"

"I have to go!" she cried suddenly, a pitiful choke of anguish. "I don't know how long I can hold it, and I can't risk hurting you."

At the sound of her footsteps he sprang from the floor and tried to stop her in the hallway, only to meet a pair of hands splitting into barbed pincers as black and shimmering as crude oil. She pushed him viciously, cutting into his chest, and he went sprawling into the bedroom where he crawled into the corner by his nightstand. The thought of hurting her sent shockwaves through his guts, but if it came to that...

"Lily, please!"

"Can't you see?" She cried, holding up her hands, the delicate skin of her wrists already blackening, transforming into that chitinous shell. "I can't be with you. I can't even be *near* you. Not like this. I'll hurt you."

"You won't hurt me," he fought.

"I will. You don't know the hunger."

Crying, she fell to her knees and crawled to him on changing flesh, clicking along the floor like an oversize cockroach. "I don't want to hurt you. I love you!"

Consumed by purest love for a soul even more damned than his own, he took her into his arms and slowly reached for the nightstand drawer.

He felt her face against his chest like a mass of wriggling snakes and he knew she was changing, returning to that cursed form.

"Lily," he said, producing the gun and solidifying his grip, wrapping his finger around the trigger in stoic anticipation. "Don't be afraid. This was meant for me, but it can help us both now."

Suddenly there was a deep, pinching pain on his stomach, and he felt warmth spreading with the red on his shirt. When next he looked, the hideous creature had him in its mandibles, tearing deep into his innards.

"*I looove you*," came the shrill cry of despair, bubbling through the waste pouring from his perforated bowels.

"I love you," he said, and placed the barrel against the shell of what was once her head. The concussive blast nearly deafened him that close space, spraying heat and unspeakable matter onto his face. Before her silent body had finished its jerking convulsions, he raised the gun to his own temple. "Today was the best day…with you," he said, and pulled the trigger.

He set the manuscript on the nightstand and settled back. Her grip on him had grown uncomfortably tight on the final page, and now he took her hand in his own and brought it to his lips.

"Are you sure you're okay with this?" he said, kissing the slender fingers. "I mean—"

She put a finger to his lips. "It was incredible. You're a wonderful writer, and your boss knows it just as I do. It's your dream."

"But this…it's so personal. I just want it to be okay with you."

"It is," she said softly. "I'm overjoyed that they want to publish your work. Besides, it's not like it's true to anyone but us. It's a shame you had to go for such a dark ending, but I love it."

"Well, it can't be an entirely true story. But you're right, there's no one that knows. No one to think it's anything other than pure fiction."

"What about Nigel?"

"What about him?"

"There's just so little of him left. I'm afraid," she said, looking downcast as her stomach rumbled like an oncoming storm. Even she did not yet know that she would soon be eating for one more.

"We'll figure something out, sweetheart. I always will, for you. I love you."

She looked longingly into his eyes. "I love you, too."

He kissed her gently on the lips then turned off the bedside light. Shrouded in silence and secrets, they held each other close.

Two hearts in the dark.

The Suffering

He sat alone in a dark room, fingers atremble before the cruel silence screaming from his phone. There was no memory of how long, no knowledge of when the call that would free him might arrive, only the sick anticipation and the dread of waiting, soaked in need and stretched taught by a lover's anxiety.

Six months. Six enchanted months they had been lost eye deep in one another. It had gone by so fast, a jumbled mess now of passionate embraces, tender clenches, whispers so loving the angels wept, and an uncountable measure of *I love you*s.

Space, she had said.

Of what meaning, of what consequence or substance was *space* between two hearts bound together by deepest tenderness? It was only pain. Space and distance were only the suffering of a face untouched, a back unrubbed, lips unkissed. So why did she want it?

Four months of the most indescribable joy and euphoria of a love so unrestricted, then she fell ill. Suddenly, with frightening force, it was as though the life had been taken from her by some devious thief. It frightened him to a puddle. He spent nights at her bedside, tending to her exhausted state, taking only moments from her to bring water or fresh clothes. She lost all appetite, all desire for anything but sleep and moaning. Some awful pain had vised her with intractable jaws, and when she hurt, he hurt worse. For he loved her with a might so fierce, he would sooner slit his wrists than see her in pain.

Despite her desires to stay with him, to be in his comfortable glow of concern and tending, he made the decision to take her to the hospital. When the tests were run and the charts read, the doctor had no simple answer. She was fatigued and anemic, losing weight quickly, experiencing pains without cause. It was decided that she should be admitted for observation. He stayed with her for days, agonizing with her, cradling his heavy head as nurses bustled between doorways and ever-beeping machines.

One nurse in particular seemed to be the one thing for which she wished to open her eyes. A young man, spring-shoed and gentle in his care of her, seemed to accord her an energy for which there was no explanation. When he arrived, she became like a new person, wholly different and renewed with vigor.

And the man watched it all with impotent consternation, wondering what was happening before his very eyes. This young, spirited caregiver was imbuing strength where he could not, and it ripped him to shreds to think of his love, his dearest heart, relying on another for comfort and regeneration.

That was when she took a bad turn and had to be moved to ICU. That's when she mentioned it and the doctors said perhaps it was best for her.

Space.

So he left and sat in her home—their home—where he had been since his arrival, and curled on the shape of her in the bed where they'd lied together on so many rapturous nights. Nights where he'd learned to caress with ravenous grace her every breach and cleft, where he had tasted eons of pleasure in mere moments that stretched into forever in her arms.

There, he sat in that darkness, silent but for his staggered, spasmodic weeping, heart wailing for his love with all the fury of a tsunami crashing ashore until at long last the call lit his phone.

He arrived and made his way directly to her. No stops, no distractions, not a single peripheral thought in the world until he was in her room on the fifth floor.

She was in bed with her eyes closed. On the table beside her was a beautiful floral bouquet in a heavy porcelain vase. When he entered, a look of pain knotted her gorgeous visage and he pounced to her side.

He reached out to graze his tips along her perfect, delicate flesh. "Darling," he whispered.

Her eyes fluttered open and her hand instantly withdrew from his.

Shaking with concern, he pressed forward. "Dearest, what's wrong?"

"No," she sputtered, her voice weak and almost afraid. "Just...I feel ill. Can you back up just a little."

"Of course," he said, stepping back quickly. "Beautiful flowers. From family?"

Heavy silence for a moment as she tried not to meet his gaze. "A friend."

"Darling, I'm scared. I've been waiting sick to my stomach just to see you. Please tell me what's going on. Have the doctors learned anything?"

"No," she replied. "I have."

A furrow knotted his brow as awaited her explanation.

"How did you get here?"

"I walked."

"No, I mean...how did you come to me? When you first arrived."

"I flew, of course. I took the first flight I could get. Remember that first evening together? It was so amazing. I so nervous," he couldn't help but smile at the memory, "but I didn't want to let it show."

"Do you remember the flight?"

"Sure." He thought for a moment. "But it wasn't particularly memorable. All that was on my mind was you. I was so afraid, so anxious to meet you in person."

"How did we meet?"

"Sweetheart, you're scaring me. You know how we met. Don't you remember the night I messaged you?"

"Yes, but how did you find me?"

"Your profile, you know this. You were so frustrated with— don't you remember? I know you do."

"You didn't have a profile, though."

"I didn't need one. I messaged you on instinct, I guess you'd say. I just felt drawn to you. We were drawn to each other."

"Do you remember any other profiles? Any other women?"

"Darling, why in the world would I even think about any other woman. You're all I want. You're worrying me so very much. I want all of your worries to be over. That's why I'm here. You were so very lonely. Don't you remember? Your heart was aching out for someone. For connection and love, just like mine."

"I remember," she said tearfully. Lunette shards of light quivered in the jewels of her eyes. "It's why I summoned you."

"Baby, you could be delirious. What are saying? You didn't have to summon me. I came here for you. Because I love you."

"No," her voice broke again and she closed her eyes to him. "No, you didn't. I wanted someone to love me, who wanted all of me. I wanted a love that yearned to drink me in like I was life itself."

His voice broke, too. "You are my life. My everything. Everything I do now is for you and *us*."

"Yes, but in the wrong way. I was lonely...so lonely. I just wanted someone. I fell in love with the idea of you, and that's what you became to me. This amazing thing that couldn't be real."

"Stop it! You're scaring me so badly right now. I *am* real. I'm *here!*" He searched for the words that might sooth her suffering, but every word seemed to scorch her like a hot iron. "And I love you. I want to give everything to you. Why did this have to happen? It was all so perfect. We've been so *happy*."

"You weren't real before I did it. Before I said the prayer and pulled you into the world with my loneliness."

He stepped toward her, flinching as she twitched with a spasm of pain, and spoke as calmly as he could to comfort her. "Darling, my love...I saw your profile. We messaged for weeks, falling in love with one another. *You* asked me to come to you. You said I made you happy, that I was a part of your soul."

"I know all that."

"Then you know how we met. I was on the first plane out—"

"From where?"

"Who cares where? Does it matter? You know all of this but what does it mean? I was nowhere without you. I was *nobody* before you. Nothing in this world has any gravity before us. I came here to start a life with you. You told me you loved me before I ever arrived, so what is wrong?"

She was so distraught, so stricken by pain and grief; she could only speak above a whisper. "You don't remember where you came from because you didn't come from anywhere. You don't remember how you got here because you just appeared. In the coat you're wearing now, with nothing else. No identification, no history, no life to check on back home because there is no back home. Because you really were nothing before. I was so very lonely, so terribly hurt. My soul was screaming out for someone to see me and love me for who I am. Someone to build a future with. It's what I wanted so badly it hurt."

"*I* see you! *I* love you! We've talked so much about the future. I'm here! We're building it right now."

"No, we aren't. Because we have no future."

He felt as though his blood had congealed to granite hardness and then exploded throughout his entire body. "What are you saying?"

"I'm so sorry. You're the one that's doing this to me. You're what's making me sick. You're hurting me."

"Oh, my love. I would never! Ever, ever, ever in a million years, until the stars burn out and after I swear I would never hurt you!"

"But you are. You can't think of it, can't realize it because you're bound. Locked by the wish I made. But you know it's true.

"Baby, you're not well. You're talking nonsense. Let me take care of you, please. Just give it time."

She closed her big, magnificent eyes. "I untie you…"

"Darling?"

"I unbind you…"

"Sweetheart, stop it, please!"

"I release you from my heart and from your purpose. You are not my love and I release you now."

She opened her eyes and gasped in awe, both captivated and terrified by his horrific beauty.

He looked at the window and saw himself as she did. He was not a man.

In the place of his fingers were curved, chitinous talons, obsidian dark, for hooking onto warm, comforting flesh and never letting go.

His face had become that of the most pitiful being. Hair sloughed away, cheeks as hollowed out caves beneath the sunken bowls of his pitch black eyes that showed neither light nor life, only pain and yearning. His teeth were jagged and black, ending in wicked points.

His coat tore and bony appendages curved up from his back. They opened slowly, revealing sheets of pale, veiny, leathery skin stretched between them. A demon's wings.

His cry of anguish was so great, so mournful, that it made her very bones ache.

"Why?" he pleaded to know. "What kind of wretched creature am I? Why would you create this?"

"I'm sorry," she said tearfully, trying not to look at the awful thing of her making. "I was so alone."

"*I was alone! I was nothing!* I was longing, yearning for this life, but I was asleep in the cradling nothingness of the void. I had no knowledge of love or pain. I was an ignorant, blissful fly buzzing between the strands of this...this...*melancholy*! This utter *desolation*! The mournful cry of the unloved! Now I *ache* as I've never known before. My chest heaves but I cannot breathe! My mind will not calm and my body spasms without cease! I have lied awake every night thinking only of you! And this is your doing? For all the love I was meant to give you, *this* is what I become?"

"I'm sorry. It's what happens when you love someone fiercely. Just as I wanted. You didn't know."

"I do love you! You are my all, my heart and my life. I would give you everything of me at your very call! You loved me, as well. You haven't forgotten that you love me. Impossible!"

"I did...I tried. But that time is over. I don't—I don't love you anymore."

He arched back in pain, grabbing his head to contain the thunder reverberating through his mind, and palmed two fresh black horns which had sprouted from his forehead. He was changing even then, becoming less human with each agonizing breath.

"We can have more times! We can make more, just us. I want more time with you. I want to give you all of my time. *Time*! What meaning is in that word now? Time doesn't end. So how can it be *over*? We loved intensely and that time both stretched into eternity and ended in a blink. How can you throw that away as nothing? Our time was passionate beyond measure! It was special, full of such love and wonder. Does that mean so little to you?"

"It was special. It was wonderful. I wouldn't take it back for anything...but I don't have those feelings now."

"*Feelings?*" He sucked air in rasping heaves. "Is that the core of this dreadful nightmare? To summon another's love to you by feelings? Feelings that come and go like the rain? That flee like loneliness at a lover's voice. What fickle, absurd *impermanence* are feelings! And these *feelings*, you've put them now into someone else? When our dream is shattered and my purpose served? Is there nothing sacred at all in the love we shared?"

"It was special to me. It always will be. I didn't mean for it to happen. Any of it. I'm so sorry that I hurt you. I didn't mean for there to be so much hurt. I just want you to be okay. I want you to be free."

"Then *love* me! End this curse! Let us be free of it together, and I will give you the heart and love you desire. I will *adore* you as I have since I first looked into your eyes. Make your love mine and mine alone and I will crawl upon broken glass for you! You will never fear another night alone. I will be your *pet* and your *pillar*. Only say you love me and I will pull down the stars just for you. You will be the Empress of all of me and the love we share will be like no other. Let us save each other from this pain. I love you! Only say that you love me, as well. I will warm you with the fire of my heart forever if you only say the words."

He fell to his knees at her bedside, the horror and beauty of his inhuman form plain to her petrified sight. His eyes were lightless orbs, his skin the color of a dead sky. His visage held all the agonized countenance of an angel impaled on the gates of despair.

She shut her eyes tightly to his plea, the very plea she had made which had brought him to shaking, terrible life. "I can't."

Her core ached with the pain of wishing that he would simply be gone. She would toss him into the tempest of despair from which she had snatched him, and it lit her every ligament with sorrow. No one deserved that suffering, and yet all would come to it in time. Some beings had no business loving so hard, but love was a disease that lovers only wished to spread.

"Maybe there is someone else—"

"*No*! No. There is nothing about you that can be paved over. Nothing to be torn to shreds like refuse and built anew. You are the foundation. You are my heart. I was nothing before you and how am I anything without you? You gave me wonderful, vibrant life. Life with love as its very bones!"

"But you are alive now! You can be free to live on your own without me! There are so many things out there."

"And *none* of them can compare to you! To what we've shared! To the rapture and warmth you put in the cold hollow of my being."

"You can live," she persisted. "You can find that again."

"How? Look at me! Look at what I've become! This pain, this love and torment has revealed me for what I truly am. A fragile, shapeless thing with no substance or strength of my own. My hideous, pitiable being has been revealed in true."

He tore aside the breast of his shirt and began to beat—*Thump!* *Thump! Thump!*—on the pale, marble smooth chest beneath until cracks webbed beneath his knuckles and spread.

"*Stop!*" she shrieked.

Upon the final blow, his fist broke through to a cavernous hollow, and the pieces of him fell away like eggshell.

"Look at me," he said, woe pouring from his every word as he let the fragments of his core fall from his fingers. "I am but dust. The world will never accept this. How could anyone else love such a miserable wretch? Your warm heart, the caress of your perfect hands, your boundless love...those are what made me alive and human. You brought me from the numb madness of nothingness where I was decaying alone. You said I was the other half of your soul! Remember the words, I beg of you!"

Even as he spoke, he saw the life flowing still faster from her weakening body. Now he could see it in undulating waves, flowing into him. Her presence, her attention, her time; all food to sustain him and his own agony.

He was the reason she was suffering, and he saw it then with such terrible clarity. He was killing her, draining her life force with his very presence. Where her body and heart needed to live on free and happy, he was the leech taking all for himself.

"Tell me what power, what magic you used to rip me from the nether. Tell me and I will use it to reverse this terrible agony of being separated from your love. I will turn back time. I will return your *feelings* and hold them dear to me forever!"

She shook her head, tears flinging from her eyes. "It was only for me. I don't even remember how it happened. I just said the prayer for you with all of my hurting heart...and you appeared."

"Then wish me back to nothingness! I can't stand this pain, can't bear this agony for another moment, let alone a lifetime!" He fell apart completely, breaking into the most horrific, stilted sobs of something that would never be whole, never be okay again. "Take back what you've done to me or I will die a slow and agonizing death away from you. Look at me...look at what I am!"

"Kiss me, then," she said so softly. "Take me, fill yourself with me. I do love you. Not as I did, but only as I can now. You were so kind and wonderful to me when I needed, when it was all I wanted. I really did want to give you everything. All of me. You served me so patiently. You gave me warmth when I was cold, you gave me all the love I could ask for."

"And I will do that forever! Only say that your heart will be mine again as mine belongs to you!"

"I can't give you my heart...I know I did once. That was what I felt at the time, but it doesn't belong to you now. I can only give you the love I feel for our time together. I can only give you my sorrow for making you hurt. I love you, but I cannot love you as you wish. As we once loved. I'm sorry."

At her words and the knowledge that she would give that to him and it would be her end, that there was no light, nor hope or victory to be won, a tremendous terror and agony of utmost finality assailed him through and through. It was a hell unlike any he could imagine.

"*Noooooo!*" He bellowed, the thunderous roar of his chest cracking open like a tidal wave against a rocky shore. It burst like thunder through his ghastly form. Unable to bear the sight and thought of it, he snatched up the vase and heaved it with his entirety. The window shattered with a crunchy, sharp *pop* and rained twinkling stars to the street below.

"I refuse to accept it! A heart *cannot* simply close like that forever! After the love, the joy, all that we shared! If you really feel nothing now, you're less human than I."

"I'm so sorry," she whispered, the trail of her clear tears now mirroring his tears of black.

"Love has the power to overcome. We can break this curse together. You can live on, healthy and happy, and I can return from this monstrosity I've become. If we love real love, pure and unreserved for the tender mercy of the other. Isn't that what everyone in life most desires? Let go of your doubts. Abandon your sense of *feelings* and just open your heart."

She did not speak, did not cry. She only lied there, trembling and shaking her beautiful, heavy head. Tears, more than words, said all that could be said, and he felt as though his soul, brought thrashing into the light like a newborn, had been swept away as dust into the wind.

She had closed her eyes to the shattering glass and the rushing gust of cold night air that filled the room. When she opened them, they marveled to see that some of his hideous form had diminished. A faint tone had filled his face, the stone hard edges of his features had softened ever so slightly, and his eyes, though still black, had become smaller and more human.

"I may not be a man," he said, his voice bloated and heavy with sorrow and regret, "but I am not a monster…and I love you so very much. I would rather suffer a thousand burns than to see you sweat a drop in discomfort. I would suffocate in agonizing torment for you to breathe freely and I would slaughter armies to see you safe. You have done this to me, left this to me, *made this of me*, and I would love you all over again knowing this pain was in store. But I will not hurt you. I would rather live a life miserable and alone than harm you with my very presence. I will leave for you. Wherever I go, whatever loneliness holds tight to me for all time. I will suffer, I will carry on…and you will live happily."

"No," she whimpered, realizing the dawn of the decision rising in his black eyes.

He ran for the window, and the world slowed to a frozen crawl. He closed his eyes to embrace the cold, dark air and felt a heaving beat deep in his chest, the broken pulse of a heart knowing the true agony of love and sacrifice for the first time. The limestone pallor and hardness of his skin filled with soft and fleshy color. The talons of his hands cracked apart and smooth, simple fingers broke free. His wings, beautiful and terrifying, stretched back fully to lift him into the sky began as they began to peel and flake away, falling to a trail of ashes in his path.

She screamed, but he heard nothing as his soft, human toes sprung him through the window frame and he opened his arms wide to be borne into the night.

Cliffert

In the desolation of The Green, time was a cruel joke.

Eons under a blazing sun. Endless hours as a punching bag for sheets of beating rain. Nights spent weeping in the cold embrace of autumn's windy affections.

Why had God forsaken him there? For what reason was that husk of existence left to rot like unloved fruit on a withered vine?

Ever since Papa-man stopped coming to see him. No more visits, no more yelling, no more hosing his funny fluid onto the corn sometimes to moans of some burning pain.

For the longest time now it was just Cliffert, riddled with the holes chewed through him by despair and the Crow-men. He was shattered and lonely, but not alone.

His only companions were the Crow-men of the Corvid Clan. Sly, vicious blackguards they were.

His left eye-button still hung on a tattered strip of his face, compliments of one of the shiny black reprobates. Spiky tufts of his guts poked through holes torn by their wretched beaks, their tools of torture and pain.

Abusive pricks. Their vain, indulgent laughter could split your teeth. If Cliffert had any, they would have been worn to gums by now.

Spiders and caterpillars and God only knew what else crawled and turned and nested in his crunchy viscera. Was it his curse to be forever home to the disgusting lesser beings which fed his reprehensible company of pitch-cloaked despoilers? To be the warmth and shelter of pests while he himself enjoyed no such comforts?

He missed Papa-man.

"Cliffert, yer such a dumbshiet," Papa-man would say, then sometimes when he moved exceptionally funny, he'd mumble into a near-empty bottle barely intelligible things like, "Why'd ya have tuh go'n die on meh?" while wiping water from his eye-buttons.

Papa-man did nothing—*could* do nothing—to stop the hurt, but at least he was there. At least he was family.

Family provided warmth.

Though Cliffert, in his own fragmented reality, understood that the Green and the Gold were a cornfield—though the how and why and any other qualifying inquiries escaped him—he had come to think of it as an emerald sea in the heat of summer, for he could not assess the steady wooshing roar in the distance with its sporadic explosions of sounds, like a mighty horn or piercing squeal. He sometimes imagined that while he drifted in place, great ships of whale hunters cut through the Green just over the horizon.

The loneliness was like being unanchored and adrift, separate from all things with no rock on which to cling. Sanity, stability, hope; these were the empty, fleeting dreams of a fragile mind.

He talked to himself, but that was no good. Why ask himself how he was doing when he already knew?

He talked to the moon, but it just smiled like a smug bastard, free to float in the sky while Cliffert was stuck on his post in the hell of the Green.

He even, in his loneliest moments when the blades of silence and neglect flayed him raw, tried to talk to the crow-men. Tried to ply their hearts with tender attention, to give them something to chew on that didn't leave him shrieking in agony. He begged for understanding.

They rebuffed his supplications with pernicious grace. *"Caw, asshole! Caw!"*

Cliffert had the vague understanding that his insides were straw, that he did not eat or speak as the crow-men did. He knew that his existence was one of being eternally frozen in place, forced to endure the endless observation of a world in which he had no value, use, or substance. He knew these things in an abstract way, but he did not know what they *meant!* He only knew that he felt pain and suffering, loneliness and despair as the seasons passed slowly, the Green turning to Gold and then finally to Grey. Heat of summer beat down on him and the cold of winter burnt his unmoving fingers with its merciless touch, and all he could do was hang there cruciform, praying for some respite.

It was a torment he wouldn't wish on his worst enemy. Not even a crow.

In the immensity of his suffering, time was merely an endless succession of days when Cliffert dreamed of giving up, of a way for him to send his mind floating off on the wind to join the stars. He wailed internally, gnashed nonexistent teeth. He bade God for surcease of the misery of such acute isolation. Some days he was so bloated with suffering he screamed into the void and heard only cruel silence in reply.

Why, God? he questioned. *Why have I been left to suffer alone? Am I so wretched that I should never see another face without a beak or hear voice instead of a sinister caw? Am I allowed only loneliness, sadness, and pain? If only I knew, if I could just understand, perhaps it could bring ease to this awful life. If only I knew there was some reason, some purpose to it all. Pain without purpose, that's true Hell.*

At last, if he should not die, if he should go on for some reason translated only through fate, then he prayed that he at least be granted the grace of a single friend. And in a brilliant moment in the middle of one of those abysmal days, his prayers were answered—in a measure—by a voice as gentle as a slushing brook and refreshing as a cool breeze.

The little song in a dress came slipping through the Green, an explorer of a strange world, and gasped in awe when she entered his dumpy little clearing.

Hello! Cliffert greeted her. *Hi there!* He knew she would not respond. No one ever did. Though he had sometimes chattered on relentlessly in the company of the Papa-man, it only vaguely played at the periphery of his consciousness that perhaps no one talked to him because no one could hear him.

The girl looked at the floating spread of him for a moment, uneased and unsure, glanced back the way she came, then slowly explored his clearing further. The Papa-man's old stool still sat nearby, turned over now by the occasion of some heavy wind. The stool were a large butt used to sag while the old man drank from a bottle and sucked on little white bones that glowed at their tips. Though Cliffert couldn't count the days (he always lost track) he could remember with bittersweet clarity the last time Papa-man sat there, looking unwell as he wheezed little curses.

The girl righted the stool before Cliffort and climbed up to inspect him, squinting at something upon him. Something below that he could not see. Her hands were on him for balance and though pain shot through his insides because it was his spider-infested, crow eaten guts that she was pushing on, he felt swell of such happiness to finally feel something new and wonderful.

Her eye buttons were such clear and striking blue, as finely calibrated as God's own sky. She was perfect, even with the bloated purple patch on her left cheekbone.

"Cl—Cliffert," she said, the lowered herself back to the ground.

She knows my name! Says it funny, but she knows!

The only thing that matched the height of his instant of joy was the weight of his constant sorrow, which for that moment, however fleeting, had been lifted like a veil of clouds.

"Bobbi Mae! Momma's callin'! I ain't movin' yer stuff all bah mahself, neither! I—holeee shiet! Lookit this ol' boy."

The sinewy, tank-topped boy that swaggered into the clearing talked like Papa-man. Cliffert first felt comfort at the jagged tune, but a bilious discontent took over as his view of the boy—and the way he treated the girl—became more clear.

"No need to be yowlin', Finch" Bobbi Mae said. "I told ya I thought I saw something. He looks so creepy."

Cree-pee? Cliffert thought.

"He *looks* like he'd make good kindling."

"*Nuh-uh*! I'mma fix him up. So don't go sneakin' yer smokes around him."

This seemed to upset the boy.

"I told you to *shut ehp* about that 'fore I sock you one again!"

Bobbi Mae backed away quickly, eyes cast to the ground.

"I'll leave yer boyfriend alone. We'll need more than your face to scare off the wildlife, anyhow. Now git back to the house!"

Sadness came crashing down again when she disappeared into the Green, but Cliffert did not lose faith. This was a sign. He believed that he would see her again.

"Do them things ever actually work?" he heard Bobbi Mae ask before the stalks closed in around her and Finch.

"Hell should I know?"

She looked back quickly and snatched her brother's arm. "Finch, look! His hand! See him waving?"

"Bobbie Mae, ye stupid—ugh! It's just the wind, girl. Now come on, 'fore Momma starts hollerin'."

The next few days were an eternity for Cliffert, and just as the crow-men returned with their beaks shined and sharpened for supper, and despair gripped him with cold, bony fingers…she reappeared swinging a sowing kit and a large hay bag.

The time that followed was at once the happiest, yet most painful he'd ever known. She tended to him from head to whatever. She stuffed his deflated cavities with fresh straw as he wailed in agony at each thrust of her hand. Feeling her reach inside of him was the sweetest pain he'd ever felt, like fire through his every inch.

She tore away his bottom half, and he beheld in horror that his legs had become little more than tattered, empty tubes of denim. Those also she stuffed with hay and with needle and thread, reaffixed them to his body. Even through the pain of this awful waking surgery, he was feeling better, more complete. It wasn't just straw that was filling him, it was affection for his tender new friend.

She fixed the strip where his eye-button hung and he could see her clearly!

A ragged hole existed where once one of the crow-men had given him vicious kisses and ripped open his stitching, and after all of that abuse, Cliffert's head was lopsided and droll. Bobbi Mae crumpled and shoved handfuls of hay into his flapping maw and though it felt like a million spikes driving into his skull, seeing the energy and care in her eyes made it all worth it.

"I envy you sometimes, Cliffert."

Why? What could such a pathetic life have worthy of envy?

"You got no one to bug ya."

No one to talk to.

"No one to cuss at ya."

No one to laugh with.

"Nobody pickin' on ya and bein' rotten all the time."

No one to forgive and make memories with.

"Nobody to hurt ya over and over, nobody expectin' ya to be happy when you ain't."

No one to hold. No closeness. No love.

They both sighed and said in unison, "You're so lucky."

"At least," she said, wiping her eyes, "we got each other."

Such elation filled the spaces between his every straw. He felt puffed with vigor and joy and...something else. He wanted his incredible new friend to stay with him forever. He wanted to protect her, to heal her, to do all the things she'd done for him.

"I know I sound so ungrateful. Like a terrible person."

You're not terrible at all. You're such a wonderful person.

"I know I have things to be thankful for. I have people and I love my family. I just feel so alone sometimes."

I feel alone all the time. Until I see you.

"I get so sad."

You've made me so happy.

"I just wish I could run away."

I wish you could stay with me forever.

"Sometimes I just—"

You're so special.

"I wish that—"

I have to tell you.

"Someone loved me."

I love you.

When his head was refilled and she held up the needle and thread, he knew instinctively what was in store. More white-hot pain, but he was ready and willing to endure it to see her happy with her work. She was making something of him that at long last had a purpose.

And so he hung and screamed and cried as she worked the needle through and through, pulling it up and down across his face. When it was finally through and he shook and laughed and cried, his stitched smile was as grand as her toothy one.

Finally, he had felt a pain worth knowing. A Hell worth roasting over for the value of love. Her presence filled him with a power that warmed him gave him what he had never known before.

Peace.

"Well looky here! Fixed old bag-face up for homecoming, did ya?"

Finch came strutting toward Cliffert with a slight tip to his step as he took a swig from a pilfered beer can.

"He looks so good," Bobbi Mae said with pride.

"Looks like somebody took a dump in a sandbag and stitched a face on it."

"Hush up, would ya? Is complainin' all you know how to do anymore?"

"Ah, screw you and your sack of crap boyfriend," Finch said. He tipped the can back to fill his mouth, then launched a foamy spray of suds onto Cliffert, hitting Bobbi Mae in the process. Bobbi Mae simply stood, awestruck at the cruelty of her kin, until Finch pulled a lighter from his pocket.

"Let's see how he looks as a redhead."

"*Staahhp!*" Bobbi Mae screamed, jumping from the stool and charging at her brother. "Why you gotta be *so mean*. Why're you such a mis'r'ble *jerk?*"

"'Cause I hate this damn place! And I hate corn! And I hate you!" He slapped her hard, knocking her to the ground. "You spend all your time mopin' around, not being sweet to yer family. Out here messin' with this pile a dogshit."

Cliffert cried out in agony, not just at his beloved friend's pain, but at his impotence to stop it.

"He's been better to me than you ever have," Bobbie Mae sniffled, "and he's just straw dummy!"

Okay, that hurt.

"You're the dummy," Finch said, and spit on her dress.

Bobbi Mae ran off toward the house, hollering. "Momma! Momma!"

"Yeah, yeah. Go own'n yell fer Momma. Whiny lil' bitch."

"Momma!"

It was some hours in the middle of an otherwise quiet night when Cliffert heard the heart-rending shriek fill the air.

"Mommawakeup! Wakeupwakeupplease! Pleeeease, Momma!"

It was the scream of Bobbi Mae, and at once all of Cliffert was alive and alight with eager concern. The anguished cry for her mother gave way to another ear-piercing squall that rolled out over the sleeping Green and faded to nothing.

Cliffert tried as he had so many times before, trying to will himself to move. *Why?* again he assailed the heavens. Why was he cursed with this heavy, pointless life of observance and loneliness? Why was he shown a glimpse of friendship and family and love only to have it denied by his powerlessness? Why. Couldn't. He. Just. *Move!*

Another scream, and the slamming of a door. Cliffert waited. Had he lungs to breathe, he would have been trying to hold his adrenaline fueled huffing at bay. For his own silence he was grateful, as he strained to listen. Somewhere far away he heard the patter of small feet.

"*Help! Help me!*" It was Bobbi Mae. Her cries split the night, and Cliffert begged every star and pleaded with the moon to keep her safe.

"Ain't nowhere to go, sister!" He heard Finch call out, and then Bobbi Mae burst into the clearing, chest heaving with exertion. Her eyes were blazing balls of blue fire, her face bloodless and grey with terror.

Why are you here? Cliffert begged to know, but he had a terrible intuition. *You must run! Get away from here!*

But where would she go? At his back lay only the endless rows of the Green. She would surely become lost and collapse of exhaustion before ever reaching help. And the other way...Cliffert knew what evil was there. The one that was no doubt at her heels.

"Where you runnin' tuh, Bobbi Mae?" Finch hollered, words slurred and angry. "Ain't nothin' out there! Momma ain't helpin' anybody no more."

Bobbi Mae looked all around, even looked up at the stars in panic, and threw herself to the base of Cliffert's post. "Please God, please God, please," she prayed.

Lotsa luck with that, Cliffert though bitterly. He cast a hateful look at that cruel joke called Heaven. *Don't waste your time.*

As if something above had heard and wanted to taunt him further, Finch suddenly emerged from the Green, a stain of beery vomit on his white tank top. The long butcher knife in his hand bore a shiny red coat.

In his face, Cliffert saw hatred so pure it sent tremors through his mind. He wailed laments for Bobbi Mae. Her brother, her family, all one should be able to count on in this cruel and lonely world, had committed ultimate and final betrayal, and what he would do next...

Bobbi Mae gagged in shock. *"How—how could you! Why!"* she screamed.

Finch wiped a wrist over the clear sheen on his chin. "Ah, it wouldn't make no differ'n if I told you. Momma always loved you best. Bet Daddy woulda, too, if he'd bothered tuh stay. But I won't be troubled with ya anymore. I'll go it on mah own. We all make it through this world on our own! Any nobody got no one!"

"You're my brother! You're blood! I loved you—we loved you!"

She sprung from the ground, scooping up the stool in her small hands, and tried to rush him. Finch was older and taller than his prey, however, and handled her assault with ease. He tossed the stool aside and took her in his arms.

"We loved you," she said weakly, tears pouring down her face, "and you hurt us."

Finch's eyes softened slightly. "Ya ain't old enough to know'ny better. I'm glad you never will be. That's just what people you love do to you."

He stuck the knife between her ribs.

Nooooooooo!

Neither Cliffert nor Finch had time or presence of mind to process or understand what happened next. For Cliffert, it was like suddenly entering a dream, as his limbs filled with life all at once and he sprang from his cross-plank post.

It happened too fast for Finch's mind to notice at first. The dark figure hitting the ground, standing up straight, then crossing the distance in just a few great strides. Finch, knee deep in his bloody business of fratricide, looked up and was instantly shocked by the freezing waters of disbelief. Bobbi Mae's body slid off the knife and fell to the ground. She gasped when she saw Cliffert, believing him to be an angel sent to lift her into the stars above.

Instead, what she saw made her scream.

Large, straw filled glove-hands clapped over Finch's head, and the boy's pajama bottoms turned dark and sucked to his leg, drenched in urine.

"N-no..." Finch stuttered, at first in shock and then in unbelievable pain, as he dropped the blade and tried with all his might to pry the hands free from his aching skull. As the pressure increased, the cry that came from his lean body was one of pure, bloodcurdling horror.

You betrayed family! You betrayed an angel! Cliffert roared and squeezed until the boy's eye-buttons turned red and the red oozed from his holes, gushed like a fountain from his nostrils and mouth, bubbling over his lips.

I'll never let you hurt her again. Because she's...MY...FRIEND!

There was the sound of crackling, and the face became a red strip between Cliffert's hands, and soon the body ceased to fight.

After that, Cliffert let the one body fall to the ground, knelt to the ground beside it, and scooped Bobbi Mae into his arms.

Please don't go! He begged. *Pleasepleaseplease!*

Bobbi Mae croaked, "Cli-Cliff-eeert?" Her voice came weak and faint from a mouth filled with blood.

He won't hurt you again. Just tell me what to do! I...I can help you! Just like you helped me! That's what friends do.

Blood splattered mumbles fell from her lips as Cliffert raised his face to the starry vault.

Have I not suffered enough for you? he screamed with every tattered inch. *Haven't I taken the endless days in this awful hell, pecked and abused until I begged for the end? Didn't I hang on that post, wailing enough to earn some shred of happiness? I've been here alone, waiting for someone, anyone to see something in me worth loving! And the minute she comes along I can't move, can't say what should be said, can't do what should be done! And like that she's snatched away from me! Is that enough for you to show me something worth all this pain? Is that enough to earn a scrap of happiness for once? So many days alone... always alone! Have I not cried enough, cursed enough, hurt enough for something good! Show me something! Give her back, you bastard! Take my life for hers! I will gladly make that sacrifice because she showed me love. Put me back upon that spike, let all within me die and give her life!*

A laughing breeze whistled between the stars.

Knowing he would receive no answers nor help, Cliffert turned his attention back to the poor girl and tried to think (a skill at which he was not terribly adept) and all that was in his mind was how he could not lose her. Not his best friend, the only person who had cared for him. He wouldn't abandon her as he'd been abandoned. After all she'd done for him, spending all that time re-stuffing his empty husk and—

That's it! I'll fix you like you fixed me! He tore a hole in his shirt and grabbed a handful of his guts—dry, sharp straw—and shoved it into her mouth. She immediately shook her head and spit his golden meat into the air.

His insides fell to the ground, now stained red.

Stop! I'm helping you! Please stop! He scooped up the fallen straw, taking a handful of dirt in the process, and shoved it back into her face, forcing it between her resistant lips. Before she could expunge it again, he made special effort to cram it as far back as he could, then quickly seized another handful of himself and did it again.

I know it hurts. It hurt me, too, but you'll be all better. Just let me help you and you'll be right as rain in no time. And we can be best friends! We'll laugh all day and watch the stars all night! We'll run and…and we'll leave this stupid field and the ugly crow-men behind for good! It'll be just us, and it will be so great!

He held her tightly to him to stifle her squirming and flailing, and felt the brittle pops of her stuffing. The poor thing just hadn't been made well. He would fix that. It was already working. She was calming, ceasing her resistance and allowing him to do his work.

He took more hay and shoved it into the slit in her chest, hoping to stop more of the red stuff from escaping her.

Now he could do his work more quickly. She knew he was helping her, he was certain of it. That's why she let her body go slack, why her eyes rolled up in relief before the lids dropped closed. She was resting while he made her all new.

He cried through the agony of excavating himself. She was littered with bits of him now, lying back so peacefully. What was left of his middle was spilling out and he would be empty there soon, so he ripped open a pant leg and took his golden sinew from there to continue his grisly, life-saving work.

Soon, he thought, glancing up at the night sky, dark and clear. *Soon I'll have a family. We'll be the best family ever, and we'll love every second and never abandon each other, and Ol' Cliffert won't be alone anymore.*

Strings

Mr. Spinley's Hearts and Stars sat at the halfway point on Grove Street, between Munson & Sons Bookkeeping and Snappy Tap Liquors. It was an old-fashioned joint, stocked with classics like jump ropes, checkers, hoops, rocking horses, hand-crafted fabric dolls, and other assorted knick-knackery for the young and young-at-heart. A display near the window held stock of a panoply of treats like Tops candy canes, sour lemon drops, raspberry Razzlers, butterscotch chews, root beer barrels, licorice bites, and more, which daily set a child's mouth to watering from across the street.

That day, Staley Cooper's mouth was dry as the desert floor as the soles of her shoes beat concrete like the drums of apocalypse. *Whoomp whoomp whoomp!* was the song of her lungs burning as the wind lifted her boyish cut hair from the pale forehead above her faintly freckled nose.

She was huffing, heaving with exertion and every glance behind revealed to her terror that they still followed. Dogged classmates, ones she'd once called friends, with no motive in the world but sheer cruelty, as hard and plain as the day was long. If only they could feel the real pain of those they tormented, would their hearts feel any amount of love or mercy?

Staley didn't have time to ruminate on such a deep question. She made a hard turn onto Grove and nearly ended up running on her forehead when she met with a shin-high barricade of newspapers and magazines being unloaded before the local newsstand.

Springing over a stack of current events, she used the momentum to propel herself faster to the doorway she sought, hoping there was enough distance to her pursuers that she might disappear successfully.

Sweating, scared, and nearly out of fuel, she ducked into the Hearts and Stars.

It was under the candy display just inside the door that Staley Cooper waited that day, hunkered down and panting, shirt sodden with sweat, trying not to mistake the thundering thud of hard rubber on concrete with that of her heart blasting like a stereo-speaker against her ribcage.

"You wanna be a boy?" one of them shouted as their hunting party ran by. Mostly likely the alpha punk; their revered leader Dennis Fegan. "We'll treat you like a boy!"

A mind can be as cruel as any person, and the voices in Staley's mind could be such awful things.

Let 'em treat you like a boy. Maybe it'll toughen you up. Her mother's words spoken in a devil's tone.

Don't even know what you are, maybe they can sort you out so ma and pa don't have to suffer the indignity of having an it *for a child.*

Just hide, another voice implored. Softer, weaker. *Just hide and pray to disappear. No one wants to know you, anyway.*

"Don't listen to 'em, kid."

She turned her head to see the old man himself, more compact than most and long arms that reached his knees, walking down his personal staircase behind the counter. "Kids can be...pretty cruel. Believe me, I know."

Staley's reply was simple and harsher than she'd meant to sound. "*People* are pretty cruel."

Sadness stared her right in the face as Spinley retrieved a bright red strip of licorice from a jar and tipped it to her in offer. "You're too young to be that disappointed in the world. Enjoy life while you can, that sorrow will be waiting down the road."

She took the gift from his somewhat elongated, oddly simian hand. "My dad says when it comes to disappointment, it's best to start young."

Staley had to avert her eyes when the heartbreak registered on the geezer's face. The shame she felt for provoking it in such a sweet man was short lived and replaced by a moment of terror as bell above the shop door sounded just behind her.

With frozen doe eyes, she spun like a top, expecting to find them standing there, pounding their meaty knuckles into sweaty palms that itched for the sticky feel of blood. Instead, there was a figure dressed head to toe in black. The collar of his coat was so high and the forward brim of his hat so low, it took a moment to understand that much of the shrouded person's face was covered in bandages beneath his dark, cotton armet. One gloved hand held a large, rectangular leather case.

At the entrance of this curious stranger, Mr. Spinley's focus shifted so abruptly that young Staley felt as though she weren't there at all. It was a familiar feeling with which she was all too comfortable. The sting of it, regardless of circumstances, never entirely faded. Invisibility did, however, provide a measure of observatory insulation, so she popped the licorice between her lips and watched the two men as though they were aged gunfighters meeting for one last high noon.

"What a pleasant surprise," Spinley said, his tone indicating otherwise.

"I hope I'm not interrupting," the stranger said. "I was simply wondering if you had reflected further on my offer?"

"I have, in fact," Spinley scratched his whiskered chin. "I've no desire to be rude, but I have to be forward. As I said before, I just don't think your merchandise is the right fit for my store. I have to stand by that. I just don't see them lighting up a child's eyes with wonder. Honestly, they don't imbue me with any sense of joy at all, and I'm about as old a child as they come."

"Perhaps you're looking too hard with your own eyes. These items are so much more than how they look. Not everything is supposed to evoke joy or laughter."

"They say laughter is the best medicine."

"And sometimes it's merely the best mask."

Spinley reeled slightly, as if faced with something awful and ugly he'd rather not see, a truth he'd rather not know. "Look, I provide gifts—"

"For the young at heart, as the sign outside declares. A charming sentiment."

"Young at heart, pure at heart. Even the lonely at heart."

This seemed to revitalize the stranger. "The lonely at heart. Interesting choice of words. You know," the bandaged face turned slowly toward Staley, who looked on in bewildered silence. "A lonely heart is a heart in need. I've always believed that each heart has a voice. If you know how to listen, you can even hear them cry out."

"Oh, I agree. And I think lonely hearts cry out the loudest."

"Indeed. The cry of a lonely heart—a shattered heart—is one of the most anguished of wails."

Spinley's eyes softened and he smiled at the stranger. "This may sound silly, but I feel like many of the adults who come through my door have hearts that are crying out for something. Simpler times, perhaps. The joy of a childhood memory. The taste of a root beer barrel or the feel of a toy they knew long ago. We lose so much in the trials of life. I think we all cry out for simple comforts from time to time."

The dark stranger seemed to have taken a sudden interest in Staley. He leaned in close until she could almost feel the breath coming through his bandages. "Do you believe that, young lady?"

"What, sir?"

"That lonely hearts cry out?"

The girl gulped, pulling the half-eaten licorice from her mouth. "I, uh...I guess I don't know."

"That's good. People who think they know are usually fooling themselves. What's far more powerful in life is what you *believe*. After the genius of youth, you'll realize you never really knew that much after all. You'll also come to realize that the less you know, the more you *believe*."

"Wise words," Spinley conceited to the man he didn't seem to like. "Sad but true."

"Sadness holds much truth." His tone turned deeper, heavier. "But a word of advice. Be careful letting your heart cry out too loudly. You never know what might hear."

Spinley didn't appear to enjoy such ominous thoughts. "You're quite an odd fella. May I ask, if it isn't too rude, why you're bandaged?"

The man stood up straight. "An unfortunate accident. You see, I was born with a face so putrid, it gave my own mother the collywobbles. In trying to remedy the unfortunate situation of not being able to look at her own child, she ended up making it worse."

At this comment and Spinley's furrowed brow of dissatisfaction, out from Staley's mouth popped a nervous and awkward giggle. She scrambled to lock a hand over her lips but it was too late. "I'm sorry," she said through a muzzle of fingers.

"Oh, not at all, young lady. I do the same thing. If we can't laugh at our own fates, we've lost sight of the real comedy...the Grand Joke in all its melancholy. I see you're the type that can appreciate a bit unease. I hope that serves you well." The man suddenly lifted the brown leather case and set it upon Spinley's counter. "I won't take up any more of your precious time, sir. I will, however, be honored to leave you with this."

"I've already told you that I'm not interested, friend. I can't see a person walking in that door and choosing these ugly things."

"Perhaps sometimes *we're* the chosen. In any case, they're free of charge," the man replied as he headed for the door.

Spinley's face expressed sudden surprise and mild offense. "Sir, my store is neither a landfill nor a thrift shop. Take your case or its going right in the dumpster."

"You do that if it's your wish. Consider it a gift. Good day to you, sir." The man looked at Staley, the deep, sharpness of his eyes locking with the sadness of hers. "A true pleasure meeting you, young lady. You should go home before you find what you're looking for."

With that, he was out the door and was gone.

"What a strange man," Spinley said with a shake of his head.

"I kinda liked him." Staley said and rested an arm on the counter, "So...what's inside?"

"Some marionettes he was trying to sell me. Came in a few days ago with them and a few other little knickknacks. Skull and bug shaped things. Ugly, each and all. I didn't like anything about them. Those hideous shapes and awful expressions. Toys aren't supposed to make you feel unsettled. They're supposed to bring joy. Whoever made the ones in this case, I'm willing to be there was no joy in them. I'll set it out back and if he doesn't return to claim it, off with the trash it will go."

"But—"

"Shouldn't you be getting home? I'd say the ruffians are probably long gone."

Staley could take a hint, even from a shaky old man. "Yes, sir. Thank you again."

"Any time. And don't worry about those boys."

"I just don't know why people are so cruel. I wish...I wish I could make them stop."

"Well, you can't control other people, so don't put your energy into thinking like that. When you get to be my age—well, any age, really—you'll understand the most important thing to control is yourself."

"What if I can't?"

The old man frowned. "That causes people a lot of problems, but you know what my remedy is? Smiling." He retrieved a trio of palm-sized spheres from behind the counter and began to juggle effortlessly with a gently grin lifting his face. "If you can do that in the face of all that's going wrong, how bad can it be?"

"I'll try to remember that," Staley said, but she didn't smile.

"I shouldn't have been so hasty. Don't rush off. Maybe there's something here that can help. Maybe fate brought you in today to find just the thing to change everything."

"Actually, you may be right. I signed up for the school talent show today on a dare, and I have no idea what I'm going to do."

"A talent show! Wonderful!"

"Not so much."

"Well, can you juggle? No? Hmm, how about some magic tricks? Singing?"

Staley was shaking her head so much she was getting dizzy.

"Look around, sweetie. I'm sure you'll find something that will inspire you."

The phone rang in Spinley's workroom and he excused himself, leaving the girl to peruse and ponder. Her eyes, eager and curious, tried to glance around the store but were drawn back to the case the odd but interesting stranger had left. It was a single clasp design, bound in tan leather that looked worn, smooth, and welcoming to the young girl's fingers, which reached to sample it's precision.

Staley retracted her hand quickly as though scalded. She had only just grazed the leather, a touch far too short to even translate a full feeling of texture to the brain, and yet she had experienced with certainty the sensation of something abysmal—a glimpse of something hideous, almost cosmic in scope—lurking just beneath the surface. It was as if, sandwiched between the binding, a billion ropey slugs were writhing in their slime in orgasmic glee.

The clasp opened with a metallic *pop* and Staley stepped back, though the desire to see what was inside quickly overpowered the urge to retreat. With a slow, shaky hand, she reached out again and braced a finger against the case's corner. She expected another sickening sensation which never came, and so she parted the case like a great maw to reveal the contents within.

Light fell over two gorgeously terrifying wooden marionettes hanging against a red satin lining. Of what blessed tree they had been carved, she could not know, but she believed them to have been handcrafted by some tormented master.

One puppet appeared to be a demon of sorts. Pale, with little black horns and a cracked hole in its chest. The carving of its face indicated that it was laughing maniacally, though tears were present on its cheeks. The other was a very creepy looking ghostly woman in a lovely nightgown. Upon her head sat a crown of stars and her face, drawn from some terrible affliction of bottomless fear, was contorted by the most articulated terror that Staley had ever seen.

They were at once repulsive and mesmerizing.

Staley wanted them.

The stranger left them, Spinley didn't want them. The decision was made for her before it had even entered her mind.

"Let's get this out of here." Spinley snapped the case shut and snatched it away, his small body lifting away the case with surprising ease. "Find your lever with which to move the world?"

"I—I thought I'd take those."

"These monstrosities? No, my dear. Not to disrespect the craftsmanship, but these things belong in a Halloween display or the dump. They're certainly not for a nice young girl like you. Besides, I don't think a puppet show would wow a crowd these days. So what else will it be?"

Her small light of hope snuffed out, Staley backed away, irritated and once again despondent. "Nothing, sir. I have to get home. Thank you for letting me hide out."

"But—"

She was out the door and gone before the old man could say another word.

Staley arrived home to the same sound as always, a choir of silence and discontent. On most days, it was to the accompaniment of the faintest tinkling of ice from her father's whiskey glass, but today there was no such arrangement. He must have stayed later than usual at the bar.

Once upon a time she might come home to the enticing fragrance of an after school snack dancing into her nostrils to the soothing tune of the microwave. A corndog or breaded chicken poppers. Now, in the suffocating air of a deeply spavined marriage, the only aroma was that of her mother's cigarettes, nearly ash from tip to filter as the wire-haired woman sat at the kitchen table, head turned away and looking out the window as Staley slumped by.

How hard it was to swallow indifference. It was an icy snake sliding down your throat and coiling around your heart. To suffer indifference is to be bedfellows with pain.

"Don't drag your feet, sugar," she might say in a tone that was both strikingly hurtful and bare of even a crumb of emotion.

The saddest was when a person was so broken yet so strong they were able to pretend like everything was okay. When they could talk to you and laugh and look at you and make you feel not one ounce of love or affection and they could do it all with a carefree grin.

That was the grin her mother had tried to keep chiseled into her face for two years while Staley began to change, when she was no longer her mother's fair-haired sugarchild, but becoming a creature that no one seemed to care to understand or accept. As she got taller and less inclined to dress like a young lady. As her hair shortened in accordance with her own style and her legs developed under the practice of outrunning boys her age. As her knees and elbows turned to knurled notches and her face lost the cushion of its baby fat.

And where there was no acceptance, the vacuum in its place was rejection.

Like the rejected sometimes do, Staley blamed herself for the rift tearing like cheap stitching between her family. Every night she watched the routine of unity turn to a dance of apathy. As silences grew longer, as words became sharper, and faces turned harder.

In the time of childhood it seemed much too sparsely spaced to connect any visible dots until her father's drinking and her mother's illness had finally reached a zenith from which both parties could only begin to roll away from each other and themselves.

When her father walked in the door that day, Staley was in the kitchen with her mother, trying and failing to summon the words to say something about the boys chasing her. Whether it would have gotten a reaction or not, she did not know, but her silence was beginning to feel as loud as a scream, and she was beginning to realize that those willingly blind were all too often willingly deaf, as well.

He called from the foyer, "Staley, you home?"

"In here."

"Found something cool today, pardner." He entered the kitchen and lifted it onto the table.

Staley froze in the toothy face of fate.

"Fell out of the back of a garbage truck. You believe that? Had to pull over anyway 'cause an ambulance was coming up behind me, so I jumped out and grabbed off the curb."

"Bringing extra trash home now?" Her mother said, and even in her shocked state, Staley hoped they wouldn't start shouting so early.

"Oh, hush up, would ya?" Her father said, slightly sloshed. "The case ain't even scuffed too bad. But now, for what's inside—" he thumbed the latch and swung the lid open for Staley's dilated pupils to take in just what she expected to see. "*Ta da!*"

The two hauntingly beautiful marionettes hung against their satin backdrop, smiling and screaming at Staley as if to say *gotcha*.

Sometimes we're the chosen.

"Get that garbage off my dinner table," her mother said, drawing a sigh of exasperation from the Cooper patriarch.

Before he could respond and stoke a volatile flame, Staley rose from the table. "Can I have them?"

"Oh…you like 'em? I thought I'd clean up the case and see what they fetch at the flea market."

"They're beautiful. And one person's trash is—" they finished together, "another's treasure."

Her mother blew smoke at them. "Get your damn treasure out of my kitchen."

"So can I? Please, daddy?"

She knew that would do it. Though he looked hesitant, disappointed, and all the other bad things that had come to call his face home over the years, she knew his weakness was still feeling like he had his little girl. Though she experienced a pang of discomfort at exploiting that sad sentimentality, it was nothing she couldn't shove deep down inside and ignore. Her parents had taught her all about that.

"Sure, baby doll. You want 'em, they're yours."

Staley closed the case and set it off the table before her mother could become any more agitated. For the first time in so long she held a bright feeling inside. A plan was forming for the school talent show, and it brought an ease to her world where there had been only strife. Perhaps it was some stroke of fate that had delivered the case to her. It was all too much to be called that useless word *coincidence*.

She smiled faintly, trying to get carried away on warm thoughts, until her father went to the cabinet and retrieved his favorite whiskey glass.

Gone were the days of fixity and the simple comfort they afforded, and though her parents mourned her change as they would a lost child, it was not she who had murdered those days.

It was them. It was his thirst and her petty anger...and her illness.

Dinner was her sitting alone with two people; being stuck between a tornado and a tsunami, except the destructive force of each natural violence was translated into stares and nods and one-word answers.

Why can't you just love each other! She wanted to scream into their dumb, blank faces, as armies of shriveled peas and coined carrots tumbled about, annihilated in their hostile maws. She didn't understand how people could be so callous to one another. After loving, holding, giving the whole heart of each to the other. What bond was capable of bringing two people crashing into one another with all the ferocity of a maelstrom of tenderness but not strong enough to keep them from drifting asunder the moment some unpretty truth came ripping into light?

How was the face you once held—the cheeks you kissed as the sun kisses the flowers at dawn and spoke secret promises as gifts in whispers—suddenly so bad? How were the eyes you once envisioned eternity with so repulsive that it made you want to push your plate away in silent disgust?

What selfish cowardice or toxicity drove people of love once as lovely as midnight rain to quit one another with such vitriolic finality?

Why is love sticky enough to bind but not strong enough to hold?

Time and circumstance? The caustic corrosion of all things?

That was dinner time. Being trapped in a room with a nothing so big it sucked all the air from her lungs, and she sat with a stack of different foods impaled on her fork—potatoes and cubes of meat and other things from a can because she was still learning how to cook—striving to draw breath because her chest was so tight she could barely chew the bits in her mouth.

Many times it began then. The bitter scowls, the salty spurns. That evening it was her appearance that was once again the initiating subject.

"I like it short," she told her mother for a time uncounted.

"It looks like a butcher took a dull cleaver to it."

She didn't want her father to jump in, because she knew it would simply shift the venom to him, but he was properly saturated and his tongue was no longer taught. "Why don't you leave her be?"

Staley excused herself and took the case up the stairs to her room against the sounds of their bickering. Once on her bed and wiping away the first of the night's tears, she pulled the shears from her drawer and cut a knuckle's length of hair from her bangs, only worsening the choppy mess on her head.

Better to cut the hair than the skin, her dad had once told her. It was because it got dreadful hot and she wore t-shirts from the lost and found. Scars would draw eyes and questions.

Once they had retired to different corners and silence overtook the house, Staley ran her hands over the smooth leather of the case, awaiting another repulsive feeling. When it did not occur, she opened the case and carefully removed the marionettes, beginning a trial session beside her bed.

The demon was her mother and the damsel was her father.

Why are you so mean? her puppet-father said, arms flailing hysterically. *You loved me once. Look at the child we created!*

We loved each other, and sometimes we can be so cruel to those we propose to love. Her puppet-mother's head bowed.

I wish only to heal the scars we've made. Love me and I will die for you. Let us love again, and our daughter can be happy.

Yes, we can all be happy together. We love you, Staley, and we will never fight again.

Silent screams propelled her through the night. It was common to hear them in those hours, cutting each other in fits and starts. Sometimes it woke her like the anxious beasts that gave chase through her dream-wilds.

"It's because you're a goddamn *coward*!" she heard her mother scream. "A coward and a spineless nothing! You're scared of every goddamn thing!"

She could tell from her father's voice that he was already withering under her mother's verbal assault. "You don't understand," the words repeated. Words he had uttered so many times.

"I don't understand why I married such a weak, pathetic piece of trash! Scream at me, hit me, do something! Be a man, goddamn it! *Be a man*!"

She buried her face in her pillow, hands clapped like a vice over her ears. How? How could a person be so awful—so terribly *cruel*—to the one they swore to love?

Even a child.

How many? How many times had one of them walked past in the hours of the night, each on their own occasion avoiding the company of the other, waiting for their lover-turned-stranger-turned-burden to finish their turn on the bed, and seen by the dim hallway light the Rorschach tests of tear stains on Staley's pillow? How many times had they seen her shimmering eyes open and pretended she was sleeping, then shut her door or retreated without a sound?

All parents have weapons of cruelty. Some use fists. Some use scorn. Others still use neglect or the weight of impossible expectations. Hers used silence. Silence was the great flayer of love and innocence, and every soundless strike cut a deep ravine into her heart. The ghosts of regret and loneliness howled through their hollow stretches.

She spun in bed until her body resembled the form of a twisted bath towel, creases of the covers spiraling up to where she had turned and hooked the top of her headboard in some bizarre reverse crucifixion. Holding back the tears already leaking into her eyes, she pressed her face to the cold headboard to reduce the feverish heat building in her head.

"Please," she whispered, and only the dark was there to listen. "I'll do anything. Use me however you want, take whatever you want, just help me. Help me control something, *anything!*"

She rolled from the covers and dropped her feet to the breathtaking shock of an icy floor. As icy as the hearts in that home.

The moon so far from her window was full and cast a blue pallor across her small feet. She stood and walked to the square portal of that soothing glow, glancing into the corner to see the case from Spinley's with door ajar where she'd placed it. Perhaps she'd forgotten to close it fully or the clasp had broken.

Placing her hot forehead against the chill-licked pane, she breathed a canvas onto the glass and carved with her finger the universal symbol of a broken heart.

Once the sea of invective had peeled back, there was only a desert of painful quiet, and then the moan of hinges broke the night as her father's gangly shadow spilled in.

"Let's be better, Dad," she said before he could say a word. "Let's be better for her. For all of us. Let's just," moonlight shimmered in the rondure of a perfect tear, "do better."

Silence again was the reply, but she knew he wasn't trying to hurt her. Never him. When her mother lashed out from spite, her father's silence was merely a symptom. Not a weapon. His silence wasn't to hurt anyone, but to protect himself.

Heavy, clunking steps (why did he have his boots on?) as he entered and sat on her bed, smoothing her now cool sheets with a rough hand.

"I can't do it anymore, sweetie."

Her voice quivered, but she didn't turn so as to spare him the sight of her tear-streaked face. "Why?"

"Because some things can't be fixed. Everything can be broken, but some things…some damn things just can't fit back together."

Her head snapped away from the glass. This wasn't her father. He was the sweetly sentimental type, always with a veneer of hope glazed over his acres of sadness. He kept a silver lining in his pocket, always for her. They were the ones that kept each other sane through the toughest times, when her mother couldn't look at either of them without a leer on her face. When things broke against walls and police had to be called to sometimes take her away.

"That's not you. Why would you say something so sad? What's wrong?"

His voice was so pitifully weak she had to take a step forward just to hear him finish. "—ust can do it anymore. I think…"

"No," Staley whispered.

"I think I need to go get my head straight. I can't take another second of it or she's gonna kill me."

"No! No, she wouldn't do that! I know it's hard, but she wouldn't really hurt us!"

"I don't mean it like that, Stales. I mean—God, it's hard to explain it to you—it's dangerous for me to be here right now. She's wore me down, baby. I'm scraped out to the raw center and I'm scared. And I can't…" he cursed under his breath. He *never* cursed in front of her. "I can't take you with me."

Staley's world fell out from under her. Words, if there were any left within her after the excavation, would not come. It felt like all the guts in her belly were lodged in her throat. For the first time she saw him with all the armor of fatherhood stripped away. His shoulders sloped in defeated arcs, caving into his chest. Finally, the nebbish created by the pain of an atrophied life was revealed in all its pitiful horror.

She dove across the bed, snatching that frailty between her fists.

"I gotta go, baby. I *got* tuh go."

"No you don't," Staley cried, tears soaking the shirtsleeve gripped like a mountain ledge in her fingers. "You don't have to give up. You don't have to stop *trying!*"

"I pray you'll forgive me one day, but if you can't, I hope you'll at least understand. Some things are just too hard. Even for the strongest, and I'm not the strongest. It's just too hard."

"Like living with me? Huh! Like dealing with a daughter like *me?* Because I'm too different? Too weird! Isn't that it? Because you two didn't have the perfect family you wanted? Well *you don't always get what you want! That's why you have to fight!*"

"Stop yelling."

"*Why?* Being quiet won't keep you here."

He sighed. "It's not you. Don't talk like that. You know it isn't you."

"She hates me! How can it not be?"

"She's not well. I'm not, either. Maybe none of us, are. Nobody blames you, baby. I blame *us* for what happened to you."

"Nothing *happened* to me, Dad! I changed! People *change!*"

"Yes, baby. People change. Sometimes they become so different you don't recognize them. Sometimes they stop loving you...and you stop loving them."

"No!"

"Shh, what was that? From the closet. Must be rats back again."

"I don't care about the *fucking rats!*"

He pried her fingers from his shirt and stood up. "I can't take it from you, too. Not you. I can't stay here, Stales. All I can say is I'm sorry."

"Sleep on the couch!" She pressed on. "Sleep in here! Just *don't go!*"

"I have to!" he shouted back, finally. "I can't take the goddamn yellin' and screamin' at me anymore! I don't want this! I never wanted this! You're not my daughter anymore, Stales. I tried my best. I swear, I tried. I tried to love your mom. I worked hard! I tried to keep it together, but she's not her and you're not you! I don't know what the hell you are!"

The last fragile thread inside her snapped like piano wire, plucked by the gleefully cruel hand of despair. "*Goddamn you!*" she screamed, hands flying to grip both sides of her head as if to stop a great wave of sadness from spilling out with her brains surfing atop.

The look of grave and sudden hurt on her father's face signaled the arrival of something; a palpable crackling of the now frigid cold air. When that look faded from pain to resignation, a soft breeze blew through from the direction of the closed window and his next look became one of intense unease.

"Stales."

She heard nothing. Her hands, now balled into fists, beat down on her legs with the fury of her words. "You are a coward! *I hate you! Just go!*"

Her closet doors flung open suddenly, smacking the walls so hard the wood around their hinges splintered and blasted apart. Staley, brimming with the froth of desperation and caught in the numb-minded squeeze of a nightmare from which she could not awaken, was unable to register the impossibility of what happened next.

"Staley, get out!" her father cried just before his body froze and his eyes, which once held the shining blue sky of a hopeful, loving father, shot wide with unfathomable terror.

They were so slender, gleaming in the moonlight like the finest webs of some rare spider. Strings, razor thin and colorless, yet gleaming with a sort of ethereal glow, reached out of the closet, undulating like snake spines until they wrapped around her father's wrists and throat, whereupon they drew tight and straight, connecting him to the dark void before them.

Staley, lost in the unreality of what she now thought must surely be a dream, could barely find her voice through the fear plucking at her every nerve. "Daddy?"

He was unable to speak, could not budge an inch of flesh. His feet were lead, his mouth held by some invisible apparatus in a frozen scream. His eyed, bulged out in some unexpressed agony like eggs from a chickens ass, barely contained a flood of tears that began to drip from their seals.

Forced by impotent fear to look away, Staley looked where her eyes were drawn by some magnetic force; to the corner of her room where the case sat fully open, the marionettes inside hanging with faces that were inanimate yet somehow brimming with life.

"Let him go!" Staley screamed

They looked on.

"Oh my—"

Staley whipped her head back to find her mother standing in the doorway, eyes saucered with fear and mouth agape, guarded by a nicotine yellow fence of bony fingers. The dingy nightgown dangling from her sallow flesh was adorned with a spreading dark stain at the crotch.

Young Staley sounded with all the tragic hope that her piercing shriek might wake her—might wake them all—from this bizarre and sudden nightmare. "Mommy!" was her saving word, but her mother was already fleeing to the stairway, feet dripping yellow and followed by the quick and devious little strings. They swam across the hardwood with all the slippery speed of vicious little eels, but it was not their malice or intent that took the legs, it was the slip of piss-covered toes at the landing which caused the elder Cooper's feet to launch with the sharpest of squeaks, carrying her haggard body into the air where she herself looked much like a flailing marionette for that one sickening moment of weightlessness.

Staley covered her eyes to the sight, but could not cover her ears, and so they heard every wretched bump and pop of her mother's journey down the steps. They even, at that distance, heard the *crunch* at the bottom that threw the world into silence.

She could not breathe, could not think, could not *feel*. All was cold and terrifying. No more words, no more screams. Her body, frozen in place, felt weak as her vision began to blur. She wished only to hug her father tight, to close her eyes and let the strings hold her, as well, and to be taken with her family to the land of the hanging dead, where they would no doubt be forced to dance forever by the hand of some cruel god.

At least they would be together.

However, her state of shock barricaded the motion in her limbs. The sanctum of her room could become her grave for all she cared, and as the world began to spin, gravity pulled her head to the covers even has her mouth hung open with an unborn scream tucked inside, and before her eyelids slid shut, she saw her father's still-standing body pulled into the darkness of the closet. Though frozen, mouth open in the middle of a silent shriek, his eyes had been alive with life.

No one was on the early, sun-baked street to see her shambling like the walking dead. The adults that would normally be rolling to their humdrum jobs in that nothing down were filing into the school to watch their little treasures perform like monkeys on a stage.

That's not to say the boulevard was empty. *They* were there, waiting.

She saw them blocking her route to the school, just outside the alley where they liked to lurk, passing cigarettes while looking for kids or small adults to hassle. It was the day of the talent show and they were no doubt waiting with predatory glee to wreak some havoc upon her with the added bonus of ruining her performance. Had she a signing voice, they would chase her until her throat went raw with exertion. Were it an instrument in her hands, they would almost certainly dash it to pieces against the concrete.

Many kids, including herself, were known to take detours around their hunting ground, but she was no longer that girl and she had not a song to silence. Her instrument was something beyond comprehension, and for that very reason she approached them without fear or hesitation, hearing the voices of her parents as they had hung before her, smiling with lifeless eyes when she had awoken after that merciless night.

We love you so much, baby. We'll never fight or neglect you again.

She walked past the dark windows of the Hearts and Stars, wondering only momentarily about the strange man with the bandaged face, and about what might have happened had the case stayed with Mr. Spinley.

Though she had no way of knowing, the ambulance on the road the day had been called when a customer found Spinley on the floor of his workshop. Cardiac arrest was listed as the cause of death.

Staley walked on.

The look on her face gave Dennis Fegan the ultimate creeps. It was not merely a lack of emotion. It was a lack of anything. He'd never seen a face so stone blank, eyes so devoid of human softness. He like softness, it was easy to squish. Her face was hard and heavy, but a weird little grin split her face as she stopped before them.

This was not the girl they'd chased just days ago.

Dennis wasn't about to let himself get freaked out by a nobody nothing *freak*, however, and the rest of the boys new that. One hand in his denim pocket, he played it icebox cool. "I'll keep it short 'cause there's something about your stupid face's irritatin' me more than usu'l. You can drop that case and run orf, or we can take it from you and then if you run. *If* you can get away."

Staley looked at them as though she's been read the lunch special. "Those my only choices? Can I have a third? Like watching you piss on a power outlet?"

"Whoa," Dean Lutz said, pawing at his crotch. "What's got into her?"

"Shut up, jagg orf!" I don't think you'll like a third choice," Dennis replied. "Unless crawling home sounds like your idear of a good time."

Staley was unmoved. "And you want my case?"

"Bitch, have you lost it? It's *my* case after I make you lick the bottom of that dumpster."

"Wouldn't you at least like to know what's inside?"

"I'll know when we're done."

"Then I guess it's time to start the show."

"You want us to hurt you right out here?"

"Don't see why not. There is something I wonder, though," she said, and popped the clasp. "Do you guys like to dance?"

"Enough of this horseshit. Get her."

She opened the case.

A sea of darkness stretched before her, little reflections like moonlight off a peaceful sea winking occasionally over the burning stage lights.

Voices from the audience *ooh*'ed and *aah*'ed as the marionettes danced to the command of her mastery. Her hands manipulated the crossbeams as though seasoned by impossible years of practice.

"One of the greatest things to have in life is someone to miss you," the demon said.

The maiden spoke with an anguished fervor that matched her tormented features. *"So many will never have that."*

"But we do. I will miss you forever as the sun misses the moon. Only be mine and all the stars between us shall be yours."

"Yes! Yes, I will! We will love as wild angels until the Heavenly fires set the universe ablaze! Until the Saints fly away with the Lord! But shall we forget our places so easily? I am only a Dreamer, and you..."

"Don't you know who I am in the story, my dear?"

"You're the villain."

"No, I'm the fool. As are you," he turned to the audience. *"As are they. We are all but fools in the Great Comedy, scurrying about in*

desperation, scrabbling for meaning and laughing at all the wrong things."

The stage to her right lit up, illuminating the four boys standing quietly. Dennis Fegan stepped forward, the strings attached to his arms and feet catching the bright light. His mouth worked open and closed while his eyes, dead and grey with cataracts, stared ahead. "I'm a fool. And a stupid idiot. And I sniff farts."

The crowd burst at the seams with raucous laughter.

The strings pulled a dead-eyed Dean Lutz forward next. "I am a fool. And it's true, he sniffs mine."

The last two followed suit with the same proclamation and their own vacuous, comedic remarks as the crowd soaked the stage with waves of guffaws.

The maiden despaired. *"What an awful fate! To be so lost and helpless in this cold, dark brutality. Listen to them laughing in pain. Laughing to cover their sadness and regret. Laughing to forget this melancholy."*

"Be at peace, my love. The greatest joke is yet to come."

"Finally," Staley whispered, reeling in the heady rush of this strange, incredible magic. All of them bowed to her whims. They would do as she commanded. No more meanness, no more hurt. No more heartbreak or cruelty. At long last, her world, once crumbling to dust all around her, was whole.

Finally, she felt in control.

She dropped the crossbars, stretched out her arms, and bowed.

And that's when the world shook. The crowd rose like a surging storm, all hands crashing together in a thunderous roar of applause while the laughter built to a frightening, shaking crescendo.

The walls trembled, the air cracked with energy.

Staley's body was overcome with a feeling of buoyancy, near weightlessness, as though all the burden of her world had been lifted from her shoulders, and with it flew something else. Something deep and integral. Without making the decision or knowing why, she looked over her right shoulder into the darkness behind the curtain and saw them; her mother, her father, and Mr. Spinley, arms moving back and forth along a strict, robotic plane, hands slapping in exuberant applause with great, wide smiles stretched tight on their faces. Their eyes were all aglitter like sparkling diamonds in the dark. So happy and full of light.

They were beautiful.

When she looked back to the audience, they had become a sea of glittering eyes, one entity emanating that bombastic, thunderous, frenzied applause! The house shook with the reverberations of their adulation.

Staley bowed again and watched a bead of sweat fall to the stage floor.

Not sweat.

This time she rose and her arms remained outspread. Her head turned slowly to the left, then to the right, her smile slowly falling away. From each of her wrists there arose a taught, clear string. Not bound to them, *part* of them.

She shivered in the cold brutality of the real. The sweet fruit of victory fell from a rotten vine, from which now bloomed rancid petals of madness. Looking out, she saw the strings shining in the air above the crowd, crisscrossing upward into the darkness like a web.

Staley stood before her adoring fans, tears streaming down her face, and laughed.

The Statement

I cannot know how this document will find its way to you. Perhaps on some damp evening you will recline comfortably your familiar space, still replete with fragile ignorance, to explore the reaches of horrifying truth within these words. Or perhaps my account may find you knocking with gentle trepidation on Death's door, a most fortuitous arrangement to make one pliant and receptive to the things herein. However the circumstances unfold, it is my wish that whosoever reads this, my abominable statement, should not immediately damn these words as the grotesque bouquet of a fertile imagination or the grimy drivel of a brain-eaten madman. This is not a trumpery tale of ethereal specters or grave-haunting ghouls meant to shock or scare for your amusement. I am leaving a testimony given with utmost conviction so that you—reader, stranger, fool—can walk with greater purpose and less hope towards a future you can now know. So that you can understand…and despair.

Where shall I begin? Birth seems self-indulgent and irrelevant. What value have I or my beginnings to anyone? I, after all, am not the important player in this document. My role is merely the messenger of a most horrid message. Perhaps I shall start at random, as sometimes nowhere is the best place for a beginning.

Imagine agony. I was dehydrated and devoured with fever in a city known more for its slime than its sympathy, lying in a gutter where stars shimmered in the feculent water. Wracked by shakes and coughs, it was day nine or ten of what could only be a serious infection of Strep. The whole sum of me was aflame, and I was alone and resigned, begging for a fast death.

The city is a hard and unforgiving creature, its cold streets and darkened alleys like the pulsing veins of a softly sleeping beast. When there seems nothing else to depend on, depend on pain.

I hope that whosoever reads these words knows nothing of such lessons and never finds occasion for instruction. The human body is such a frail heap of nerves and emotions, flaw upon flaw, grief after grief. If there is more deranged and dysfunctional creature upon the Earth, it hasn't been discovered.

How I arrived at that pitiful threshold is a sordid but altogether boring tale of my own ignoble excess, fueled by some standard contempt or another. A lover's scorn, a privilege wasted, the sweet pleasure of addiction, or any of a countless many types of self-sabotage. One was the same as another in the end, and I knew them all. It was not so much as an end, however, as a sort of genesis.

I had journeyed to a dark district near the waterfront, wishing to see the serene lights glow upon the water's face for one final night. When darkness took me in the jolly, rotten bowels of the bubbling gutter, my last hope was that it was all finally over and I would never graze the blight of another day. This was not my fate, however, as I awakened sometime later in the faint light of a single dingy bulb hanging in a brick lined cube of a room.

I was alone, but still feverish and reduced to a bed weight upon a beaten mattress on a stone floor. In time, a man entered, draped in shadows.

He introduced himself as Father Marcus Debilis. An older gentleman, frail and ashen-haired, and the strong medicine he offered brought blessed relief. His eyes were kind but lightless, and at first acquaintance my instinct was that I needed to separate myself from this oddly uncomfortable man. Despite his aid, something in the frailty of his spirit made a deep sadness swell within me. I also could not disregard the fact that I was at the mercy of a stranger who could very well have devious intentions. Being desperate and with nowhere to go, however, I decided that should he make an attempt to end my life, then my fate was already sealed.

"Where am I?"

"Underground," he replied, quickly raising a hand. "Don't be alarmed. You're not a prisoner. You're in a room in the tunnels beneath our facility. No harm will come to you, and you're free to leave at any time."

"Did you bring me here?"

"I did. I, along with the others here, do our best to help the community, namely the lost, the homeless. Those like yourself. Forgive me for being so forward, but were you prepared to die out there?"

For a moment, I was unsure if I should answer honestly, but I felt no judgment emanating from his eyes. "I suppose I was."

I expected a degree of condemnation, or some religious pageantry. Instead, I was gifted compassion and, in a manner, companionship. He brought me water for my dehydration and whiskey for my thirst. We made odd, delirious conversation, as if he had joined me in my despondency. We spoke of sad things, of the hopelessness and desperation that most keep hidden from sight. We talked of the strange hells of this world, horrifying and arousing. I found his resignation both satiating and disturbing.

"Some people think if such hell exists then surely there must be some equal measure of heaven," I philosophized with no clear point.

"Have you ever heard the term...no of course, you haven't. There's a term known as *grimdark*, conventionally used in fiction. It describes a universe where all the worst possible outcomes are real and true, and all the best possible outcomes are not. It basically embodies all our greatest fears about existence; that life moves in a constant state of pain and decay, that we are doomed to lives of torment punctuated by inevitable death and oblivion, or perhaps even inescapable Hell, with very little good in between."

"People must believe in something good for a reason," I argued, cradling futility. "They hold on to hope when all else is lost."

"People," Debilis said in disgust. "People will extol every value of hope until it's something they think you shouldn't hope for. Have you ever noticed that hope is a magical star lighting every sky, until you hope for someone to come back to you? Think about the worst pain and agony you've ever known, the worst you have ever experienced, the moment you thought most fervently of ending your life. You hope. You hold on. You *survive*. Now... imagine you have a child, and for your child it goes the other way, they don't get better or they don't survive or they just give up. Would you believe the unmitigated garbage that *people* spew then? Would you believe in hope or anything else?"

I felt it impossible to answer at the time, and though I had lived in the breadth of hopelessness for quite some time, a part of me thought the man insane.

"Have you ever been stricken to tears, to staggering, chest-wracking sobs by something so powerful it overtakes you completely? Some serene, beautiful song? Lyrics that spoke pure truth to your soul? A sunset or night sky so deep, so vibrant, you couldn't help but break down?"

"That's quite a way of putting it, but yes. Yes, I'd say that I have."

"When you looked through your tears into the center of all that feeling—the center of everything—and saw the universe unfolding outward in glowing lines of brilliance, did you see at it's very middle, in the atom of all you've ever known, anything that made you feel *hope?*"

My answer was immediate and sharp. "No."

He leaned back, apparently calmed by my reply. "That doesn't mean that I've given up," I quickly amended. "Hope is more than a solid state. It ebbs and flows. Some days are harder than others, but every day has an eventual end."

"And how did you come to find yourself face down on the precipice of oblivion?"

"I don't claim to be strong. In the moment, I didn't care to go on any longer."

"And now? Has your suffering lessened to the degree that hope springs back?"

I didn't reply. I could not, for I didn't even know the answer, myself. I knew that I was tired but afraid, clasped tight by the fear that had always held me close.

"How did you know?" I asked. "About the moments when I see it all; the universe unfolding, the lines of brilliant light all glimmering like…"

"Like a web."

"You've seen it, too?"

He offered nothing in reply, but stood from where he'd sat down beside me. "If you're not going to stay, you should get further medical assistance. You're dehydrated and sick. If you should ever find yourself free of this plague called *hope* and want to see the truth rotting beneath the flesh of the world, you're always welcome here. I can show you what's in the shadows, where most refuse to look. But if you return, you must be truly unfettered, unchained, and unleashed. If you should come to feel that hope is a lie, there is a place here for you."

I was once incarcerated in a prison with a graveyard in a lone corner of the yard where prisoners were buried with little unmarked white stones over their graves. They were the bodies of people whom had spent most of their lives in prison. Some of them didn't even have names, arrested as vagrants and derelicts with no documentation or recoverable history. They were the graves of bastard children who entered the system as kids and never made it out. They died without family, without hope, without basic literacy. Imagine what they went through. Imagine a life of that much pain and futility. Imagine...a life destined to go to waste.

I was reminded of those poor souls, and I felt as though I knew exactly what Debilis was talking about. I was sure he knew a great many things about the tragedy of life.

He led me upwards, out of what I learned was a network of labyrinthine tunnels beneath our feet. Back at sea level, I emerged from what turned out to be a small and rather decrepit brick building tucked into the city's ass crack. He told me that it was a refuge for the forsaken, the broken, those bankrupt of life and hope, like myself. While I was too disoriented at the time to give it much thought, I suppose I realized then that I was not in a conventional church and Debilis was not a priest.

My parole officer during a time long past was the type of man that tried to force optimism down your throat. Happiness was a choice, and everywhere he saw a world of people too stupid, weak, or lazy to accept and make happiness for themselves. He was a real disciple of the Church of the Bootstrap, so to speak. At that time, I was the hardest case he'd ever met. I told him at every turn, mostly from a desire to irritate his sensibilities but also a profound conviction I did not fully understand, that the world was a miserable cesspool of disappointment.

That the people you love will betray you.

That you will wish your life was merely a dream.

That you will wake suddenly in the shadowy afternoon of life, wailing in the afterbirth of some terrible revelation.

That all of your dreams will crumble, and all of your hopes will be destroyed.

He said I was an idiot. That people like me didn't deserve the life we were granted and that I was a waste of oxygen and resources. He said if I hated life so much, I should just murder myself.

I saw him many years later in a run-down dive where I occasionally hung with other low-lives. He was alone and sallow and I'd never seen a face undergo such a transformation.

"You were right," he said.

I paid for his drink and left.

Debilis had called a cab take me to the nearest hospital. As I got in, I looked back at his clear, lucid eyes. He said, "Thank me when you return."

Dear Reader, whomever you may be, whatever heartache or affliction has gripped you in this life, I wish I could inform you that I fled that haven of surrender and despondency to heal, to rise, to take control of my destiny and climb to new heights of happiness. I wish that I could tell you that the spirit did overcome, and that like so many worse off than myself, I found the strength to fight on for glory and honor.

However, I am no such liar. A dullard, a coward, and a useless husk I may be, but I will not spin an uplifting tale to spare you from the sorrow of a foul resolution.

It is not to say I did not try. All of my life has been trying. Trying to rise, trying to be more. Trying with might...and failing. How torturous to reach upward and outward only, at so many interludes, to be smacked down by that which we cannot overcome.

Though, with aid, my physical sickness dissipated, the sicknesses within me have rooted far too deep to be ripped out. My addiction, my hopelessness; these were pits from which I could not ascend.

In time, I was in danger of ending up back on the streets. My mother, to whom I was closest in this world, succumbed to her own illness and died in a care facility. When I received word, I knew then that there was truly no fuel left to stoke the fire of life. I was a heap of dying embers, with nowhere left to turn.

So I returned to Father Debilis on a night when thunder crashed and fulgent, coruscating jags of purple lightning cracked the sky over the roaring harbor. All of the heavens were being ripped asunder over my head, and I could feel some deep, troubling perturbation swelling in my chest.

Eaten with collywobbles, I fled into the building and asked for Debilis.

Once reacquainted, I settled into my final home and Debilis welcomed me with open arms.

"It's time you understood who we are," he said. "Walk with me."

He led me through a dizzying maze of tunnels and corridors, at every few junctures taking stairs further underground.

"Do you ever think about luck? Fate? The invisible hand reaching out to trip or gift us at any moment?"

"Don't we all at some point?"

"Have you ever considered its inherent connection with human suffering? How, like the concept of luck, a malignant...*melancholy* churns with the very fabric of creation. Have you ever felt that there was something looming over all things? A shadow, a veil, something personified by this tragedy that has befallen us all."

"God?"

"Something...parallel to God, or what we think of as God."

"I'm afraid I don't understand. I don't know this 'shadow' is or what it has to do with me. What tragedy?"

"The tragedy of our knowledge that all we are, that all the pain and indignity of human frailty is endured out of pure coincidence."

"You're talking existentialism. No meaning, no purpose. Sounds like the ultimate freedom to me."

He stared me down. "And what have you done then with your freedom? What countless pleasures you must have experienced without boundaries or limits. Tell me of your endless dream. Go on. Tell me about the paradise of pleasure without consequence you left to rejoin us here."

I swallowed, shaken by his sudden fervor. "I'm just saying—"

"There *is* no freedom! Is it your freedom to choose how you'll suffer today? Or only what you'll tell yourself to make each moment bearable? *We believe* that an awakening can end this terrible charade of human folly and suffering. Not just for us, but for all innocent lives yet to live. No one should be ripped away from the sweet embrace of nothingness to endure this…grinder. *We* are the things that *should not be*."

"That's weakness. I don't believe that."

"Do you believe that you came to be here by coincidence?"

"I came under my own power."

"For what reason? Why did you return where there is nothing for you? I told you to return when hope was nothing but a word that conjures bittersweet memories and nothing more. What did you come here expecting to find?"

"I...I don't know."

"I believe you do. And now it's time for you to see."

Presently, our path opened into a chamber so expansive, so crushing in the weight of its open space, that my breath caught in my chest. Like the tunnels through which we walked, much of the cavernous room was illuminated by electric lights. What generators powered these lights or where they were located, I hadn't a clue, and I was too stricken by awe and wonder to think in proper order. The chamber expressed the form of a temple of sorts. Perhaps a church carved by some ancient order long ago.

The shapes, the effortless curvatures, patterns and symbols indecipherable to my brain tessellated yard upon yard of stone. Hand-chiseled faces displayed their forever frozen rapture just for us. There was more than the eye could drink in a single gulp. The architecture was like nothing I had ever seen. I fear that to describe too much of this subterranean edifice would diminish its unfathomable magic. It could never be properly illustrated by such a feeble hand as mine.

"It's breathtaking, isn't it? Carved into the earth by hands of those yearning to express the sorrow of the soul. Imagine what black seas of infinity they saw."

Suddenly bereft of cause to doubt, I swallowed the stone in my throat. "What do I call...Him? It?"

Debilis began walking deeper into the chamber, and I aligned myself with him once again. "It is the God with No Name, but we have our own. It is the Lord of Countless Sorrows, the Weeping in the Stars. It is the Eater of Pain, the God of Torments. Master of Tears. Sometimes we call it He Who Wails for Us. There is one title we have grown quite fond of. It is...The Weaver. The Weaver of Melancholies."

I stopped, suddenly overcome with emotion, my mind reeling back. "My grandmother used to...used to say such a thing. Oh child, she would say, you're just weaving melancholies."

Debilis offered a sad smile of understanding. "Do you still believe you came here of your own accord?"

I was numb, silent, unable to formulate an answer satisfactory to myself. I was unsure of everything. Unsure and frightened and curious. "Is it the personification of our pain?"

"Perhaps, but I don't think so. I once believed it was formed by the human need to find reason in our sorrow. An egregore, of sorts. A machine wrought of our fears and weaknesses. Now I believe it is much older than us, that it predates the human condition. But I believe we sustain it, in a sense. Just as the breath of fire fills a house with smoke, so does the breath of our pain fill the void to sate and grow him in his slumber. This is the belief that I have come to after what *I* have seen. The truth, however, is that we don't know for sure."

"What you've seen?" I asked, no coursing with terrible chills. "*What* have you seen?"

"I have seen it once, along with a few select others here. Or rather, I have seen what my feeble, limited mind could comprehend and not a bit more. It was indescribable. My mind has locked it away to protect my sanity. Thinking of it is like chasing a ghost in the corner of your eye. You only know it's there, but if you look to catch it, it's gone. I saw what can never translate into human language."

I looked all around at the impossibility before my eyes, my body electrified and shaken by serene tremors. I gave it only a few moments of thought, and I didn't even need that long.

"I'm ready." I said, turning back to face Debilis. "I want to see it. I need to go where you've gone."

"Perhaps you shouldn't make a decision in haste. You can still turn back, but once you journey beyond this point—"

"Look at me. I've had all the time I need to know there's nothing in this world for me. You believe I'm here for a reason. Do you really think I'd turn and walk away now?"

"No, I don't."

"I can feel it within me now. It feels as though I'm a puzzle piece, lost and adrift all my life, finally slid into the place I belong. Tell me what you require of me and I will give it. Please, Debilis. This is where I'm supposed to be. I can *feel* it."

"Then I already know what you will say when I reveal the rest of the puzzle, when I tell you of the ritual."

"Tell me all. Withhold nothing."

Debilis took a shaky breath. "Should you join us, and undertake our endeavor, you will be taken by lift to a chamber deep beneath our feet, to one of the lowest parts of the temple where all of your questions and doubts will be laid to rest. You will enter once, and never again. What you see inside will change you. What you are now, in all of your ignorance, will be blasted away and the path will become as true to you as it has for us all. It will fade from your mind quickly, for it is too powerful to hold, but it will remain within you until the final step."

"Could it kill me? Or drive me mad?"

Debilis kept my gaze. "It may. It is different for everyone, and some minds haven't been able to take it. Those who survive without their consciousness flayed to ribbons come back with a sense of unshakable calm. A feeling of absolute certainty."

"You're saying if I survive then I won't be afraid anymore?"

"No, my friend. I'm saying that fear will be the least of your concerns."

As for my current whereabouts, I sit—for now—relaxed and comfortable in a subterranean chamber somewhere beneath the city streets, warmed by a space heater and strong drink, pouring these final thoughts onto my utmost enemy—the hungry page.

I once asked; "Why does real life have to be so ugly?" Now, I can answer for myself.

Because it's real. It's the truth. There is truth in ugliness. Beauty hides the lies.

Only look at the horror, insanity, and insatiable brutality of the world and you will see in the undercurrent all that I have relayed.

As I write this, it has been fourteen days since I spoke with Debilis in the great temple chamber. His words echo in my mind.

"If you still wish to stay and join the ritual, it will mean the end of your life as you know it. What awaits you on the other side, in the company of the Weaver, I cannot know. You will journey beyond our universe."

"Why haven't you taken it?"

"It is my hope that someday I will, but for now my duty is here. I watch over this place and welcome the broken and the hopeless. But the time approaches, my friend. Perhaps, if there is anything of our souls that remain, I may see you on the other side."

By now, dear Reader, you are no doubt wondering about what transpired. Are you aching for me to give you some glimpse of the other world? Of what dream-creatures float in the mists of the Weaver's cosmic garden? You can see it all. Everything that we are, the grand and terrible truth of creation. It is in every despicable deed, every gore-strewn scene of carnage. It is in the rotting corpses and the brutalities perpetrated by man against man. Disappointed though you may be, remember that the sick cannot always see their disease.

Yes, I entered the chamber, and Debilis was right. What I saw inside removed all doubt from my bones. I tumbled over the wheel of eternity for the span of a single moment, turned loose like a shooting star across the expanse of some great cosmic vault. I saw the writhing shape behind the stars, and my ethereal eyes burst into flame.

My mind feels calm and far away, too numb to process the terrible truth that filled me on that awful night. Now, I prepare myself for the ritual. I prepare to sacrifice myself for the mercy of the Awakening. To save every shattered heart, every lost soul. All that flesh bound to pain and debasement, bent over and bleeding jagged shards of dreams denied, yet still holding within that bitter venom called *hope*.

What drives the soul when there is naught but sorrow and despair?

This endeavor is not done out of hate. It is to free this fragile realm of skin and bone from the awful, inescapable truth. The truth I saw as I trembled in the eye of dark aether and its ancient god. It is that truth that towers at the core of my statement.

We are lost. Humanity cannot escape its tragic fate. A great maw of darkness and unspeakable horrors yawns beneath us. In that darkness there is no meaning, no redemption. In the vast empty spaces between stars we cry out, desperate souls caught like helpless flies, tangled and screaming in melancholy's web.

Zach Miller is an American author and random junk enthusiast who writes in various genres including horror, action, and suspense. He is a lover of music and food and spends his free time under the crushing weight of existential despair.

Please direct lavish praise and/or profanity-laced tirades to
ZMAuthor@gmail.com